My Grandmother Was Green

RHONDA ROSE

DEDICATION

This book is dedicated to Mary,
So that God may do His wondrous works through me.

CONTENTS

PROLOGUE

The word grandmother conjures up many images for everyone and regardless of what name you call her by, we hold dear to us our special and fond memories of love for our grandmothers.

Depending on your background, you may have called her Bubba or Baba (Eastern European), Bubbe (Yiddish), Babushuka (Russian), Babcia (Polish), Bunica (Romanian), Grandma or Nanna (English), Nonna (Italy), Grand-mère or Grand maman (French), Oma (German), Abuela (Spanish), Awa (India), Lola (Philippines) Sobo (Japanese), or Lao Lao/ Nai Nai (Chinese).

There may be many more terms of endearment, but one common word we share for our grandmothers is Love; pure, grand and awe-inspiring Love.

The love of a grandmother is like that of no other. Grandmothers have a special way of loving us for more than we are or hope to become. They see the light in our souls and love us unconditionally with a joy that parents, in all the responsibilities they have of raising us, don't have the power to see. Our grandmothers hold a special place in our lives and even those who have never met their grandmother can feel her presence deep down inside, guiding and holding them near, offering hugs and comfort in the middle of the night or in times of stress and trauma. Our grandmothers live inside of us, motivating us, allowing us to be who we were born to be, reaching out and guiding us through life's trials and tribulations. We learn so much from our grandmothers, as it is they who have laid the foundation for our lives through their countless sacrifices, hard work and love for the family. And it's with this unconditional experience of love and dedication that I share this story of a grandmother's life through her adoring granddaughter's eyes, inspiring her grandchild with her wisdom throughout the years.

I am the woman who my grandmother raised me to be. She taught me many things about the plants of the earth and their healing powers as food. She taught me not just to cook, but to appreciate food, to know it deep down inside, and to treat it as though our life depends upon it, which of course, it does.

1

WHERE IS HOME?

"Where we love is home-home that our feet may leave, but not our hearts."
-- Oliver Wendell Holmes, Sr.

You do not have a soul, you are a soul. Those were my grandmother's words that really struck home with me, quite literally changing the way I viewed myself. The body is the mechanism through which your soul does God's work.

Not really knowing where here is, I had to ask myself how I got here and what was I planning to do to get out of this place? I used to wear nice clothes, drive luxury cars and eat at fancy restaurants, but not now, not so much. As a young adult, I never thought much about the quality of the food I ate, only the taste of it and I certainly never thought about where my food came from, only that it was already made and hot, waiting for me behind the deli counter or written about tastefully in the menu from where I could order it once I decided what I was in the mood for eating. But then, the recession hit and my job at the loans company ended when the stock market took a turn for the worse. Finding myself unable to pay for my mortgage or my car lease, I was forced into living in a modest apartment in a decent part of town that was at least considered safe to be in, take public transit or walk and to start preparing my own meals. Wow, it had been such a long time since I'd cooked anything of substance for myself that I was beginning to wonder what I was going to do, how was I going to feed myself? And then, as though I'd been living in a dream, I remembered the teachings of my ancestors, those who had worked the land every day to prepare meals and build a future for their families. I thought about how my current lifestyle had abandoned all the old ways of survival and I almost became ashamed of myself for letting that happen, and for forgetting where I came from and what I was made of.

Today I'm treating myself to a glass of Riesling and a small dipping tray of pita, hummus, red pepper and eggplant garnished with green and black olives at one of my favourite hotel restaurants in Toronto where I regularly visited in my wealthier days. Listening in on the business men lunching at the nearby table, I heard the stories they were telling about people spending their money differently these days and because of that, construction projects were shutting down causing significant barriers to making money. There were no women in this crowd, but I don't know if that has anything to do with this story, just that it's an observation. Through the windows overlooking the hotel's front entrance, I saw fabulous cars like BMW's, Porsches, and Mercedes being driven into the valet parking. Handsome and well groomed men in business suits stepped from the cars and were immediately ushered into the elegant and powerful luncheon bar. "There's still money out there," I muttered quietly to myself, "It's just in the hands of only a few."

Sitting there, I watched what they ate and thought to myself that it's no wonder so many business men died of heart attacks and cancers in the prime of their business careers. The stress they encountered every day in their jobs and the food choices they made were enough to kill anyone let alone someone whose exercise routine each day consisted of walking to their valet parked cars and taking a few steps in and out of the elevator only to move from one board room meeting to another. I would hope many of these men would consider getting a gym membership or a bicycle to get out on for fresh air and exercise. Focusing back on their diet, I saw that instead of ordering the fresh homemade roasted red pepper and tomato soup or the veggie and hummus dip that was on the menu, they ordered deep fried chicken wings and short ribs as the appetizer. And for their main, they ordered fries and a burger with bacon, cheese, and mayo on it instead of choosing one of the many fresh garden salads to go with a grilled chicken breast sandwich.

Staring at my own food, I began thinking how expensive the bill was going to be and of how my grandmother would be horrified if she knew how much money I was paying for a simple glass of white wine and a few pieces of pita and three small dishes of dip. Grandma could make this food with only a few dollars and it would be healthier and tastier than what I'm eating now. But at least she would be pleased to know I was ordering what she considered to be a healthier food choice.

Growing up with Grandma, I played with Barbie dolls and dreamed of wearing beautiful clothes, of driving great cars and of having gorgeous boyfriends who absolutely loved me and only me. Oh, my younger life was a fairy tale, I know that now. The neat thing is, this fairy tale life did happen for a while, well sort of, but it didn't last. It had been equivalent to living on a bed of quick sand that was slowly sinking and soon I was to be engulfed in it by the weight of my own selfishness. I was very lucky though, to have had it for a while because it did develop life skills in me that I would otherwise never have learned. The experiences in my life taught me about humility and empathy; two things I might have lacked in my entire life had

I'd not lived through what I did.

Comparing myself to so many others in life, I know I'm blessed. Sitting here, I reflect that I found another job, a humble one, but one that pays the bills and keeps me fed with a roof over my head, and, I have my grandmother and all the skills she gave me. She gave me dreams too. I still dream of being endlessly young and of getting married and having children, but when you're in your thirties and don't have this yet, it's not likely about to come, or so I told myself repeatedly. Today, I know I'm beautiful. Only it's on the inside and not the outside as I would have thought it would be. I mean, when I asked for beauty, I had a lesson to learn about where and how beauty manifests itself. I was shallow in my wishes asking for it on the outside, when all the while, I did have extreme beauty, but it was on the inside and I had only to let it out. I exercised at a gym and participated in yoga and Pilates classes to stay fit trying to keep my figure sleek staying healthy for as long as I could. I waited for that day when the man of my dreams would come my way sweeping me off my feet; and when I saw him, I wanted him to know we were meant for each other. I wanted him to be pleased I was the one for him. I wanted him to see me inside and out and I wanted him to love it all. And, of course, I wanted the love making to be fabulous, I thought, smiling to myself. I know my wishes were not all modern day thinking, but I didn't care about that. In many ways, my thinking was retro and I liked it that way because the things I learned from my ancestors are keeping me balanced in today's modern world. What's old is new again.

Dreams are the very food lives are made from. Without dreams, life has no surrealism and no magic. Life has no growth and it has no hope. Grandma told me dreams are built on faith. She said that if I have faith, then I will dream, and if I dream, then I will have hope. I remember hearing a song when I was young that put beautiful musical lyrics together about dreaming of a better land that I assumed meant an earth different than ours now, where people worked and lived together no matter of their origin. I'd dreamt of this very same vision with this same outcome and too wondered why it couldn't come true. And then I extrapolated it to, why can't my dreams come true? Why can't I find that job that satisfies me, why can't I remain in a relationship longer than a few months and why can't I be the way I dreamed myself to be?

Grandma loved me just the way I was, I was sure of that.

She often said to me, "You are exactly as God made you and God can use you to do his work no matter where you are or what you are doing. We must always listen very carefully to His nudging and know that if you ask Him, His hand will be in everything and He will guide the outcome according to His plan giving you strength and rest along the way. Even things that detour from His plan will eventually be brought back on track if you pray for it to be His will. That is His promise to us all. He loves us and will guide us to His kingdom, but we must want to be there and we must ask for His help and then listen for His direction. Signal graces are the signs given to us letting us know He's there even when it's hidden from us, and that He's guiding us, with His hand in everything we do."

I suppose I always believed Grandma because she was content with her life and she was happy. My grandmother is the most beautiful person I know.

But as I said, I wanted to be more than content and happy; I wanted to be enthralled with my life and lively. I wanted to be enthusiastic and to live it to its fullest believing I'm in the Garden of Eden here on earth. At that moment, I envisioned the plants in the garden of Grandma's house and I saw my version of the Garden of Eden. I saw the plants growing and standing tall and strong, not shy about their leaves waving in the breeze or embarrassed by the nakedness of their stems holding the newly grown blossoms, exploding into growth and exposing its goods for all the world to see. This plant is pleased with what it holds and displays. And then I envisioned looking down at my legs and noticed how covered up I was and as I glanced my way up my body viewing my chest, I saw I was hunched over and not standing tall at all, not like the plants were. Instead, I looked more like the sunflower plant that had grown past its prime and was losing its bright sunflowers to decay, unable to hold its head up high anymore, sadly saying good bye to the world. Comparing myself to this sad looking sunflower, I realized I needed to do something about the way I was standing and I needed to do it now. I needed to exercise even more and I needed to get outside and enjoy the sunshine and perhaps take a vacation to the mountains where I could hike and become one with the land breathing in the fresh air cleaning my lungs and giving fresh oxygen to all my body parts. I needed to strengthen my upper body so my neck would be capable of holding my head up high and I needed to strengthen my core so I could stand tall and be seen as a shining pillar of light, to do God's work as He intended for me to do. Free will is such a beautiful thing when it's turned over to God to perform His miracles here on earth, "...Thy will be done on earth as it is in heaven..." as said in the Lord's Prayer, one of my favourites. Once my free will is turned over to do God's will, then I match here on earth as it is in heaven, and that became my goal when I learned my true gift was in understanding how I become nourished for good health by the land we live on, and in doing so, my body becomes a strong and healthy vessel for which God can use my strength to provide new life and guidance to others.

Plants teach me so much. It's like God is talking to me through Grandma's garden plants clearly showing me the messages He's wanting me to have. He wants to reach me and this is how He does it. Maybe I'm dreaming, but these are the dreams that can come true and for me, they're worth listening to.

Snapping out of reverie, I noticed the business men had finished their lunches and left. It's time for me to leave too. Paying the bill, I gathered my coat and said one last good-bye to this old beautiful hotel knowing that likely I would never return to it again. But I take comfort knowing I will continue to have eggplant, hummus and red pepper dips because I know how to make them. And I will serve them with my own fresh garden vegetables while drinking garden grown teas and delicate homemade wines. My name is Emerald, picked by my grandmother because Emerald means green, and green was Grandma's favourite colour and the colour of her gardens.

Hummus Dip

Ingredients

1 cup of uncooked chickpeas
3 tbsp tahini paste (sesame seed paste)
5 garlic cloves
1 tsp salt
1 tsp black pepper
5 tbsp lemon juice (preferably freshly juiced)
2 tbsp olive oil
1 tbsp olive oil spread over dip
1 tsp paprika sprinkled on top of olive oil and
A piece of fresh parsley

Instructions

1. Boil 1 cup of chickpeas until softened (about 30 minutes). This will yield two cups of cooked chickpeas. In a food processor, combine cooked chickpeas, tahini paste (sesame seed paste), garlic cloves, salt, black pepper, lemon juice (preferably freshly juiced), and olive oil.

2. Blend until smooth and pour into a serving dish. Garnish the top with

olive oil spread over dip, paprika sprinkled on top of olive oil and a piece of fresh parsley.

3. Serve chilled with pita, fresh or lightly baked with olive oil, baguette or use as a spread on sandwiches in place of butter.

Roasted Red Pepper Dip

Ingredients

3 roasted red peppers

4 cloves of garlic

1 cup of cheese from the following selection, white cheddar, parmesan, asiago, mozzarella or cream cheese. Any combination of cheese can be used

½ tsp dried mustard

1 egg

¼ cup oil such as sunflower, almond, canola or light tasting olive oil

1 tbsp lemon juice or white vinegar

1 tsp salt

Instructions

1. Preheat oven to 350 degrees Fahrenheit. In a baking pan, brown 3 red peppers at 350 degrees Fahrenheit for 45 minutes. When roasted, remove from pan and allow to cool, leaving the skins on. Only remove the skin if it has become charred or blackened. Preheat oven to 350 degrees Fahrenheit.

2. In a food processor, combine roasted red peppers, garlic, cheese, dried mustard, egg, oil, lemon juice or white vinegar, and salt.

3. Preheat oven to 350 degrees Fahrenheit. Cover and bake for 20 minutes.

4. Serve warm or cooled with crackers, pita, baguette, or vegetable slices.

Baked Artichoke Hearts Dip

Ingredients

1 egg
½ tsp salt
½ tsp black pepper
½ tsp cayenne pepper
1 tsp paprika
¼ tsp mustard powder
¼ tsp sugar
1 tbsp white vinegar
½ cup of oil such as sunflower, almond, canola or light tasting olive oil
1 cup artichoke hearts
½ cup mozzarella, asiago or white cheddar cheese, chunked or shredded
¼ cup parmesan cheese
4-6 garlic cloves
6-8 pimento stuffed olives

Instructions

1. Preheat oven to 350 degrees Fahrenheit. In a food processor, combine the following ingredients: egg, salt, black pepper, cayenne pepper, paprika, mustard powder, sugar, white vinegar, oil, artichoke hearts, cheese chunked or shredded, parmesan cheese, and garlic.

2. Pour mixture into an oven baking dish and garnish with pimento stuffed olives, or other olives. Cover and bake for 15-20 minutes or until bubbly and lightly golden brown.

3. Serve warm with crackers, pita or baguette (fresh or lightly toasted).

Variation

Add 1 cup chopped spinach before baking to make a spinach and artichoke dip.

2

THE EXQUISITE BEAUTY OF MY GRANDMOTHER

"The beauty of a woman is not in a facial mode but the true beauty in a woman is reflected in her soul." -- Audrey Hepburn

"I wouldn't put that in there like that," Grandma exclaimed, "this is how it should go in, slowly and gently."

We were making supper together and I splashed flour and water onto the back of the stove by pouring it too quickly into the boiling water while making the gravy.

"It's the gravy I like the most, Grandma. How do you make it?" I asked with my nose over the pot smelling the aroma of the herbs and spices. Gravy, I always heard, was bad for me, but this can't possibly be unhealthy. This just smells so delicious and looks so good.

"Ah yes, the gravy, Dear. This is a recipe I invented myself to get your mother and aunts and uncles to eat their vegetables. If I tell you, will you promise not to tell your mother? She has never asked for my recipe yet has always licked her plate clean whenever I've made it. It was the best way I could help her to eat nutritiously given her stubbornness and dislike for certain tastes."

And so in the spirit of continuing to cook with my grandmother and share in her recipes, I agreed to not divulge this new found information to my mother.

My mother and grandmother had a strained relationship, to say the least. I think it's true that mothers and daughters often go through tough times, but this relationship border lined crazy. I could never quite understand what fueled the fight, but I didn't want to be in the middle of it. I was certain that at some point in their lives, my mother would realize how true and humble her mother really was.

"I promise. Not a word from me," I declared my allegiance to Grandma.

"Very well, then. First, the veggies get boiled like I'm making soup. Then I blend them all to a fine puree adding cooked potato water for added nutrients. I thicken it up with flour or corn starch, whichever I have in the cupboard, and I add salt and some of my fresh garden spices for flavour and voila, the gravy is delicious."

"What about the colour, Grandma? How does it turn brown?"

It's the mushrooms, Emma. When mushrooms are boiled, they turn brown and so they will turn the gravy brown naturally. Sometimes I spoon some mushrooms out before I puree the vegetables and then I add the mushroom pieces back in so they can be seen in the gravy. I'll then add chopped green onions too. I can add some sage, rosemary or poultry seasoning to compliment the colour and flavour for what I like to eat. If I'm having chicken and I want pale gravy with a soft yellow colour to look like chicken, then I add some turmeric. The benefits of turmeric are many and help with things like digestion and inflammation, both of which I can feel great about helping my family with. And your mother, God bless her, loved this recipe."

I still remember the exquisite beauty of my grandmother. Her name was

Rosa Belle meaning Beautiful Rose. She had dark brown hair with bright green eyes, a prominent chin and strong cheekbones and she often held her head just off to the side with pride and dignity that made her look like the woman of strength that she was. There was a picture of her that my own mother kept on her writing table located in the TV room loft and every time I climbed the stairs to the loft, I saw my grandmother's eyes looking back at me with love and approval in that special way she had. Sometimes I thought this was my own reflection looking at me and then I'm reminded that it's the family resemblance showing through. I have a distance cousin who tells me often that it's my grandmother I most look like, although I find it humorous that my dad's family all think I look like him. I figure I must have both sets of genes prominently displayed in me for each side of the family to see their own genes so clearly. Talking about this, I'm reminded of a picture I once saw in a learning exercise at leadership camp for summer students. The teenagers at the summer camp were divided into two groups and then each person was handed a sheet of paper with a charcoal sketch on it. The picture on the sheet of paper was the same for all. In isolation, one group was told the picture is of an old lady and the other group was told the picture is of a beautiful young woman. Each student then looked at the picture until they were seeing the image of the woman as described to them. The two groups were then brought together and each person was encouraged to look at the other's picture confirming it was the same sketch as their own. Once everyone agreed they had the same picture, the councillor invited everyone to yell out at the same time what the picture was of. If one was listening in from the outside, then one would hear half the group yell out "an old lady" and the other half of the group yell out, "a beautiful young woman". It was at this time the students in the group realized something was different. They looked at each other's picture again and confirmed the picture was the same as their own, disbelieving they had seen it correctly the first time. After confirming it was indeed the same sketch, the students questioned what the difference was and soon realized the difference was in the way each person viewed the same image based on information they'd received before seeing it. I believe my family processes which of my parents I look like the most based on their view and closeness to each one of them. Those who have never seen my grandmother of course don't relate me to her at all. And since there's only a handful of living relatives today who've seen my grandma, I rarely get complimented as looking like her anymore.

As you can tell by now, I love my grandmother very deeply. Always have and always will. She and I are very close and I look to her for comfort, spiritual growth, healing, happiness and healthy recipes. The recipes that are easy to make and give real home cooked meals flare and exceptional taste are my favourites and there are so many of them. I also look at my grandmother with gratitude. It's because of her I turned my life around and became the person I am today, healthy and beautiful on the inside.

Grandma was born in 1917 in the Niagara Region of Ontario Canada during the First World War. Years later, she was to give birth to her own children during the Second World War. I was lucky enough to have been born in a time when the world as a whole was not at war. She grew up very poor but her family were hard workers and saved what little they had to ensure their eldest child could earn a living that was better than they had. They insisted she work after school hours to help earn enough money for tuition fees for school and so she managed to attend nursing school in Toronto where she boarded with a relative to save on money. She met her husband at a young age and was married at twenty two soon after she graduated. Grandpa was a civil engineer who had studied at the University of Toronto too and it was there they met during campus activities and varsity games when their two faculties joined together. Within eight years of marriage, Grandma and Grandpa had five children and Grandma spent most of her first married years nursing her own children to good health. Grandma and Grandpa had the kind of relationship everyone admired. They made friends everywhere they went, giving freely of themselves and of their possessions. During difficult times, they ensured their neighbours had enough food to eat by sharing their garden produce or by taking over hot meals to a neighbour whenever a family member was sick or the mother had just given birth to a child and Grandpa helped with small repairs around the homes of families where there was no one around who was able to do this. They built their home in Pelham near the heart of where is now known to be the region's wine making country and on land they'd received as payment from a family who Grandpa helped by building them a house. There wasn't enough cash to pay Grandpa for his services, but the family owned over a thousand acres of farming land and so they paid Grandpa by giving him two acres of land which gave them enough room to build their own modest house, grow a small garden and raise a few farm animals such as chickens, pigs, rabbits and turkeys. It was a hobby farm, Grandpa joked, but we all knew these animals were for eating and not for pets. It was from this farm that Grandma shared her food with those less fortunate than herself and she never complained about not having enough for herself or for her own family. Grandma's kindness was known all over the region and she was happy to have it that way. I remember Grandma's house as being warm and inviting with fresh smells of bread, cookies and stews in the kitchen. There was usually a pot of hot tea steeping on the stove in the afternoons and the ladies of the neighbourhood often gathered in Grandma's kitchen to share stories of their newborns and discuss local happenings such as the fair coming to town or the weekend farmers market with all its meats, breads and veggies they loved to purchase. Sometimes Grandma took her own bountiful crops such as beans and peas to the weekend market to sell but mostly she gave them away and so didn't earn much of anything, but she was happy. She felt that if she had extras, then they were meant to be shared. Southern Ontario has always been a great place to grow food with its warm summers, plenty of sunshine and enough rain to keep the grass green and the vegetation lush. Eighty degrees and green is how I grew up thinking of Ontario.

I suppose it was because of all the adventure and opportunities I had available to me in Ontario that I was inquisitive and active, which gave my parents a challenge. Today, the internet makes having a questioning child easier with all its answers at a mouse click away, but when I grew up, I had to ask people around me or read books that were available to find out the answers to my questions. I wanted to learn all I could about so many things, like how cars were built, how food was cooked, how sports were played and how to enjoy the great outdoors with all its wilderness and vast acres to discover including how to swim in those glorious lakes. But mostly, I liked to learn what other people already knew, because I liked hearing their stories. I liked the way people lit up when they recaptured their youth while telling me what they used to do. Learning stimulated my mind. It introduced me to so many people and experiences and challenged me to grow into a woman who made my grandmother pleased with her own life, knowing that it was because of her and the circumstances of her life that I was born.

We are all connected in this universe and we all affect each other in some way. For every person you reach out to, speak with and interact with, there will be many more whose lives you will touch, those who you don't even know. Just by the pure presence of your being, as those who connect with you move on to connect with others, you will be connected to one another.

3

THE MIRACLE OF BIRTH

"Until one has loved an animal, a part of one's soul remains unawakened."
-- Anatole France

I think basic wellness and nutrition came naturally to my grandmother. She had the ability to heal people and animals like no one else I knew could. She could look at a person and know they were lacking in vitamins or essential fatty oils or in some cases, were lacking in love for which she would give them her warmest hug as therapy; heart hugs, she called them, where two people hugged each other from their left sides placing their hearts over each other's. Grandma was convinced the energy from the two hearts merged supplying synergistic energy, making each person feel better. She also had a special way with animals that she translated into working with human beings and for that, she was well known. If someone had something wrong with them, she could tell what is was by looking at their eyes, skin, complexion, energy level and by listening to their words. For animals Grandma could feel their fur or look at their teeth and know the health of the animal instantly.

Grandma particularly loved cats and horses, but horses were too costly and difficult for her to keep on her small property and so she didn't own any. I remember the day I found stray cats in her shed and Grandma could tell their diet was lacking in protein, something that a cat's diet has to have lots of. Looking at the three cats, she tried to approach them, but they wouldn't allow it. Instead, they circled her and meowed with a low throaty growl clearly telling her to keep away. They would have no one near them to threaten their newly found territory.

"Leave them be, for now, Dear, they'll get used to us soon enough and once we've earned their trust, they'll let us help them. Cats are proud, cautious animals and very intelligent too. They'll learn what to expect from us once we show them a few times that we're here to help and will not harm them. For now, place the food and clean water by the door and they will come on their own terms to eat and drink."

After placing the food and water where Grandma instructed me to, she and I went on with our chores working in play time with the pigs, rabbits, and goats. Every farm seemed to have a goat and they were all named Billy. Ours was no different.

The cats were nowhere to be seen and all the while I did my chores, I glanced over at the water bowl to see if any were drinking, hoping to catch a glimpse of the gray and white one that I was sure was a male. His gray eyes had my interest because they seemed so alert and yet there was something in them that seemed to just want to close and have a long rest. He looked very tired, like he hadn't been able to relax his muscles and slumber into peace his entire life. I was sad for him because I thought if he would just let Grandma help him, he'd be able to lie by the fireplace keeping warm and safe.

"That will come, Emma,' Grandma assured me. He will see that we are good people and he will feel safe enough to trust us. He'll watch our actions for a long time to ensure we are consistent and then he will learn to trust. Once he does, he'll purr for us to show his affection and then he'll sleep warmly by the fire day and night with a full belly. He'll be relaxed once he sees he can be. Right now he's protecting the females and their territory. You will see the one is already with kittens so the food is going to her at this time. He will not eat until she has eaten. Watch them when they approach the bowl and you will see that he'll stand back and watch over them while they eat. Only if there is anything left, will he then eat."

"But what if there's nothing left?" I asked with a worried voice.

"Then he will not eat. That is how it's done in his world. Chivalry is alive and well in the stray cat world."

"If he doesn't eat, he will become weak getting sick and die, won't he Grandma?"

"Perhaps, but we won't let that happen. We'll take care of them all and they will live, including the new kittens."

And so it was to be a whole two weeks before Grandma could convince the stray cats to trust her. Hearing loud meowing from the shed, Grandma and I ran from the sitting room to see what was going on and upon opening the shed door, Grandma saw through the darkening evening light the tiniest kitten coming from her mother's womb, covered with tiny drops of blood, eyes shut tight. Grandma ran to the kitchen, grabbed some clean towels and warm water along with a old blanket and a flashlight and quickly ran back to the shed to help the mother cat deliver her kittens. Standing on the sidelines watching, I was mesmerized by the miracle of birth happening right here in this shed and yet I was scared. Scared that the mother cat or one of the baby kittens would die and scared that I wouldn't be able to help and that I would cry, making this a bad memory for all my life. But with Grandma's skill at nursing and her careful, loving nature, she helped deliver all seven kittens alive and healthy. Mother cat was tired and allowed

Grandma to help and so the bond of friendship between them was established and was never to be broken until twenty one years later when the mother cat died of old age. The kittens were adored and loved by the community and grew up close to home. It was a fairy tale of a sort, with no harm being done to the cats or to her kittens and only fond memories stayed with me. After the seven kittens were born, Grandpa took the mother cat to the vet to have her spayed so no more kittens could be born, and the vet cared for them all as a charity measure to the small town. And that is how I too, came to love cats.

4

SEPARATION AND THE GRANDCHILDREN

"Ever has it been that love knows not its own depth until the hour of separation."
-- Khalil Gibran

Grandma's own children were born without much fuss or commotion. For each one, Grandma was taken to the hospital and delivered within the day having healthy, lively babies one at a time. Twins were not part of my grandparents history and none have ever been born in either side of the family. They had two boys and three girls in the order of girl, boy, boy, girl and girl. My mother was the fourth child and second girl born to them.

"A difficult woman she was to raise," Grandma recollected, "always stubborn and defiant yet childish in her ways and had to be the center of attention at all times. She never could let the spot light shine on anyone but herself and so it didn't surprise me when she came home one day with your father and was already married. Eloped. It never occurred to her that I would want to be at her wedding or that her own father would want to walk her down the aisle. We missed so much of your mother's life because she did whatever she wanted to do and didn't think to include us in her decisions. Some say it was a blessing we had two other daughters to delight in, but it didn't make up for missing your mother. We hardly ever saw her. When you were born, she went right back to work and you were only a few weeks old. I watched over you like you were my own and fed you your bottle, rocked you to sleep each night and gave your mother updates on your first tooth, first steps, and first hair cut. It was too much for me to see your mother put her own career ahead of her family, but your father supported her and didn't mind that I was your primary caregiver during the day. It was a good thing you were an only child for so many years because honestly dear, it would have been too much for me at my age to raise both you and your brother at the same time I had Shelby living with me."

Shelby was my cousin born to my Uncle Sid and Aunt Hilda, my mother's older brother and his wife.

I didn't know what to say when anyone talked about my parents and how they were absent from my life. I knew my grandparents were always there for me. I thought my parents loved me, at least they never said anything otherwise to make me think they didn't. Sometimes it hurt and other times it didn't because I didn't think much about it, but pain is a hard thing in life and pain of the heart is the hardest of all. I remember the time when my grandmother experienced the heart wrenching feeling of being separated from her son's daughter, her other beloved granddaughter, at a very young age.

Shelby was born to my aunt and uncle around the same time I was born. Having no place of their own to call home, Grandma and Grandpa welcomed the newborn Shelby and their son and daughter in law into their home so they could raise their baby in a safe and loving environment. After years of listening to a child's laughter and giggles all day, every day, and of hearing the pitter-patter of tiny footsteps on the hard wood floors and stairs, Grandma's house went quiet on the day her beloved Shelby was ripped from her home.

"I'm leaving and I'm taking my daughter with me!" yelled the woman with the long black hair, Aunt Hilda.

I still remember that day like it was only yesterday. I had been visiting with my cousin playing the game Kerplunk on the little table in her bedroom and sipping pretend tea with the stuffed teddy bears which is something Shelby and I loved doing together. We were only seven. On that day, when I walked in, the house had an eerie feeling, one of dark heaviness that was so unlike Grandma's house. Normally everyone was happy, and the kitchen was filled with bright sunshine and great smells of baking and cooking, but today, none of that existed. Putting it out of my mind, I playfully skipped up to my cousin's bedroom to begin our afternoon of play time together. She had a bedroom filled with all kinds of toys like dolls, board games and stuffed animals and we were quite capable of using our imaginations making the most of everything and enjoying afternoons filled with dreams and make believe fantasies that left us dreaming of fairy tales and feeling like princesses each night. It was a great childhood together.

"Shelby!" the loud voice from the bottom of the stairs boomed. And then the crash at the door revealed an angry woman who looked dishevelled and very unhappy.

"Mom, what is it?" Shelby asked.

"Pack your clothes, we're getting out of here," Aunt Hilda yelled while grabbing items from Shelby's dresser drawers. Her mother started flinging socks, underwear, pants, dresses and whatever she could get her hands on, throwing them all into a pile on the floor and then ordering Shelby to pick them up, and put them into the two large garbage bags that she had brought with her.

"But where are we going? Mom, what are you doing?" Shelby began to cry.

I was getting scared. I didn't know what was happening or why and I didn't understand her mother's actions and anger, but I did know that this wasn't fun or comfortable. It seemed like a black hole was encircling my head and that I was going to lose consciousness. After grabbing all the clothes from the floor and stuffing them into the bags, Shelby's mother grabbed her arm and dragged her out of the bedroom holding the two garbage bags in her other hand. Shelby was screaming and crying and her messy hair was covering her face so I couldn't see tears, but I knew they were there. I knew Shelby was crying real tears this time, not like the fake ones she put on when she tried to make me feel bad for taking her doll or for using her hair brush.

Slam! Went the bedroom door on their way out and then loud footsteps went down the stairs and slam, went the side door. And then, silence. No one moved, no one spoke and no one dared to say a thing. All I remember was Grandma standing there, her face a shade of gray that I had never seen in my whole life until later when I grew into an adult and saw a dead person in a vampire movie. The three of us, Grandma, Uncle Sid and I, stood there for what seemed like an eternity before my uncle took the first steps to sit down on the couch. Covering his face in his hands, he began to sob. I had never seen a man cry before, but that day, my uncle had an emotional breakdown and he cried himself into such a state that he was never the same afterward. The rest of his life was spent with no job, no focus, and no love for anyone and no care in the world. He spent his days riding around on his bicycle visiting junk stores, pond shops, and garage sales. Each day he brought home mounds of unwanted items that sat at my grandmother's house collecting dust and rotting away. These were all items that I thought would likely never be sold to anyone else and would only be sent to the dump upon my uncle's departure. But later on in life, I learned I was wrong. I learned that over the years, Grandma had sold most of that stuff to pay the bills to the house that allowed her to continue living there after my grandfather's death and until her own departing day. She resourcefully restored many of the junked items and used whatever she could around the small farm selling the rest making it a recycling project of her own. After all, my grandmother was green.

I don't think Grandma ever did see Shelby again, and neither did I. It was like Shelby never existed in our family and somehow this all seemed so very wrong. Grandma hurt deeply inside and I could tell this because every time she saw a young girl with long blond locks, Grandma stopped what she was doing and stared into nothingness and I could tell she was remembering Shelby and wishing she could hold and hug her once again. But it was not to be.

Uncle Sid eventually moved out of Grandma and Grandpa's house, but his mental health deteriorated over the loss of his family. Grandma couldn't convince Uncle Sid to care for himself and so Uncle Sid disappeared from Pelham without a forwarding address. Pain was once again residing in my grandmother's heart. She now had two children and one grandchild whom she feared she would never see again; her son, Uncle Sid, her daughter in law, Aunt Hilda, and her granddaughter, Shelby.

Grandma took mental health very seriously, connecting mind, body and spirit together. Having lived through a world war, Grandma was very well aware of how a person's state of mind and emotional well-being impacted the physical state of the body. Many times she saw how a letter from a loved one could literally change a person's whole outlook in life by cheering them up and this led to a speedier recovery of the body. Of course, Grandma was mindful of those who were seriously mentally ill, those who had been pushed too far in stress and would never recover. She prayed for all those in the hospital that they would be protected from the horrors of mental illness and that they would find mental and emotional stability in their lives. For those who she could help, Grandma ensured she gave them plenty of food with vitamin B and she helped to give them activity so their bodies would circulate 'love through their veins,' as she referred to it. I recall the first time I heard Grandma using that phrase, I didn't have a clue what she was talking about. It was much later on when I learned of the power of love that I realized Grandma was referring to the endorphins released in the body when exercising. These endorphins have the power to make a person feel good, feel alive and refreshed and to help heal the body through the emotional state. That's why when I feel down, I like to exercise and soon, I begin to feel good again. The exercising helps with circulation and that alone gets blood and nutrients flowing to my whole body.

Proper breathing techniques have been a long time passion of Grandma's. Deep breathing, healthy body postures and stretching are things Grandma did every day. I often found her lying on the floor in her living room with her arms outstretched and her knee bent up over her hip breathing deeply and filling her stomach with air. Envying her dedication to Pilates and yoga techniques, I attempted to do at least one breathing exercise each day regardless of where I was. I even learned how to breathe fully while sitting at my office desk and I believe that just by doing those simple breathing exercises, I was able to deal with so much stress that filled my working days.

Grandma had been careful to nurture her physical relationship with my Grandpa too. While I loathed to spend any time thinking about their private lives, I know it existed because they often took time to 'just be with each other'. In public, they were both very supportive of each other and held hands often, embracing that physical connection they shared together. But the places I saw the healthiest connections were in everyday conversations where the words they spoke complimented each other and encouraged one another. This led to healthy conversations where the whole family could learn how to help support another person's emotional growth. In conversing with each other, the words were carefully crafted to provide positive messages and outcomes leading to growth. Friends and family alike noticed how gentle they were with each other and how this gentleness emanated outwardly as love. Love was the key to her happiness and her health. And Grandma always took the time to love.

In addition to loving my Grandpa, Grandma loved growing herbs and 'healing' plants such as Gingko Biloba, Gotu Kola and Green Tea which she steeped in hot water and sipped throughout the day to help with her circulation. As Grandma grew old, she insisted on maintaining a vibrant circulatory system because she said that would help her to deal with the stresses of life in an 'ever changing and fast paced world'. I remember laughing at her when she first said that to me, but then I thought about it and she was right. Her generation lived from horses to cars to farm machines to electricity and televisions, to automated bank machines, to computers, to massive interconnected highways, air travel and so much more. Had a generation ever had to learn so much so quickly before? I doubt it. I suspect Grandma's generation learned the most, and the quickest. Through all her mind, body and spirit teachings, Grandma was able to deal with the anxieties of change and of being separated from her loved ones.

"While the people are absent in my physical life, they are present in my mind and in my spirit. No amount of physical separation can keep me from being with my family," Grandma told me on a day that I was missing my mother. "Gardening helps to take my mind off the bad thoughts and replaces them with good thoughts. I keep moving, getting circulation going through my veins and I start to feel good about the life forming in the plants. In the winter, I get outside in the cold crisp air by bundling up warmly and going for a walk. That helps to clear my mind and then I start to feel happier, and I like to feel happy. The blood flows through my veins faster and my body feels warmer all on its own, filling me with deep love."

It was that deep love emanating from her that I can best describe the warmth of Grandma.

5

BEACHES

"In every outthrust headland, in every curving beach, in every grain of sand there is the story of the earth." -- Rachel Carson

Grandma enjoyed going to the beach at the lake with its rushing waves, sandy shores, fresh algae smells and clear blue skies overhead. She liked seeing the birds flying around, swirling about like feathers in the air, looking for food by diving, swooshing and then grabbing small fish from the water, before flying back into the blue sky, gracefully floating in the air all the while looking for more food.

It was a treat for me to go with her to the beach on the shores of Lake Erie, carrying our sun umbrella, beach blanket, aluminum lawn chairs and picnic box. Helping us to see through the glare of the sun, she and I wore blue tinted sunglasses and tied our hair back preventing it from blowing in our faces by the cool wind that blew off the lake. Walking over the hot sand to our favourite spot, we laid out our blanket, the one that Grandma kept in the old linen closet for days just like these and then pitched our umbrella so the shade would be there covering our picnic box filled with delectable treats for the day, keeping the ice in the box from melting so quickly in the hot sun. After setting up our area, we sat on lawn chairs at the water's edge enjoying the waves rolling in. While dipping our toes in the water, we felt the wet sand rolling over our feet and then moving out again with each wave, slowly, back and forth, returning every few seconds, and repeating the motion that calmly mesmerised us. For quite some time, we soaked up the warmth of the sun on our skin with all its vitamin D filling our bodies, smelled the fresh air off the lake, felt the wind over our faces and relaxed in the sights and sounds of the great outdoors. In my adult years, I often thought back of the fun I had on those beach days with her in the sun and I could imagine feeling the breeze through my hair as if I were there again, feeling the wet sand on the shoreline squish between my toes as the waves rushed in.

The people on the beach seemed friendly enough with the children playing with their sand pails and shovels, the parents looking at them over the top pages of a favoured summer paperback and the waves rolling into shore in the background with the lake expanding well into the horizon. Everyone had windblown sun bleached hair, tanned bodies and glistening eyes with smiles wide and their voices laughed all around us. All day long, the people came and went, and on special occasions, Grandma and I were lucky enough to be able to stay with some of them well into the evening, socializing and making new friends. Bonfires on the beach at night were the best. Those were times of socializing, laughing, and cuddling under a warm blanket and storytelling. Nothing can compare to those calm star lit evenings. Looking back from my adult life filled with responsibilities, I see now that I should have spent even more time enjoying those days and less time worrying about what my future was to be since I couldn't control it anyway. My grandmother had always encouraged me to enjoy my youth as she had never had the opportunity to do so in her younger years due to the war and the lack of money in her family.

Through those shared days with her in my youth, my grandmother's love for beaches passed on to me. Remembering my teenage years, night time on the beach brought adventure and personal awareness. It was a time to leave the clothes on the sand and skinny dip into the moon lit waters of the lake. With the waves gently brushing the shore line and covering my feet as I walked slowly into the soft rolling water, my toes curled at how crisp the cool water felt sending goose bumps up my arms and hardening the nipples on my breasts and I wished for the warmth of a man instead of the cold of the water that was held in the soft waves. Knowing that after this swim, the heat of the bonfire would feel so good against my skin and would warm me on the inside, and so with this thought, I submerged my chilling body into the depths of the water only to feel that it was warmer than I had thought it would be and warmer than the star filled, moonlit night air. Splashing around, I laughed and giggled and dove into the rippled lake showing my white bottom to the stars above. I could see the eyes on the shoreline starring at me, knowing the boys could feel my existence. Walking out of the water and not shy about my nakedness, I saw them starring, yet trying to be discreet by diverting their eyes when I looked in their direction. Their conversations belied their actions and their thoughts were distracted by me as I heard in the mumbled words of approval they said upon seeing me slowly emerging from the depths of the water with swaying hips and long wet hair. I felt beautiful for a brief moment in time.

Later in life, I experienced the beaches in a different way. They were still magical and I still wore scant clothing if any at all, but these beaches were in the Caribbean where it was hot all year long and the water was the therapeutic salt ocean, green in colour instead of the fresh water of the gray-blue coloured Great Lakes. Many weeks would be spent on the Caribbean beaches soaking up the sun and occasionally being sunburned seeing my skin turning a lobster red colour. It was the rashes on my shins that caused me the most pain as it felt as though I had been burnt with hot sand and irritated with scratchy dry weeds. This, of course, is not what actually happened, but the redness on my shin was not to be ignored. There was definitely something wrong here and I had to learn how to be in the hot sunny weather without all this skin irritation.

"Zinc Oxide, Emma," Grandma's words rang in my ears. "You can make sun block for your skin very easily and cheaply and it will give you so much sun protection acting as a physical barrier between the sun and your delicate skin."

"Where do I buy that from Grandma?" I asked with interest.

"At the pharmacy," she replied. "It will come as a white powder and you can add it to your favourite skin cream just by adding three parts of cream to one part of zinc oxide powder. It will prevent your skin from burning, and it will provide protection against rashes. The funny thing is, diaper rash cream contains zinc oxide in it which is also an easy to buy ready product to protect against the sun. It will make your skin turn white, but you'll get used to looking a bit pale and it will wash off with warm soapy water. The great part is that it's mostly water resistant to cool water and so it will protect the skin while you are swimming and while you're sweating which makes it great to wear when you're outside at anytime. I like to wear it while I'm gardening because it also protects my skin against the oil from the leaves on the plants and the acidity of the soil. It helps to heal my skin. Why just last week, I was digging in and around the zucchini plant that has sharp stems holding its leaves and my forearms became scratched and red and so after I had washed my arms, I applied some zinc oxide cream and within minutes, the soothing effect of the cream made my arms feel so much better and the redness quickly went away. Come the next morning, my arms were healed."

"Does it really wash off," I asked?

"Yes, of course it washes off and with just a gentle soap and a wash cloth. Afterward I like to apply aloe juice with some added vitamin E oil to soothe my skin and give it a fresh revitalizing look. I'll fill a small bottle with aloe juice, add some vitamin E oil to it and splash it on my face, arms, legs and feet at least a couple of times a day. I love how it feels so satiny soft and my skin always looks radiant."

And with that sage advice, I never had another sun burn again and any garden rash was quickly relieved with diaper cream or as I like to think of it, with zinc oxide. Aloe and Vitamin E have become staples in my bathroom cabinet and nightly, I apply this delicate mixture to my skin for freshness and good health.

With my skin covered in the whiteness of the zinc oxide and feeling protected against the elements of the sun and heat, my grandmother and I prepared lunch on the beach for the two of us. Today, it was jerk chicken prepared with fresh garden herbs and a homemade fresh pesto and pasta salad. Oh, my mouth watered just thinking about how good that was going to taste.

"It's only eleven o'clock, Emma," Grandma teased.

"Yes it is only eleven o'clock, but we made this food last night and so I've been waiting sixteen hours to eat, and that's a long time, Grandma," I teased back.

Laughing, Grandma conceded and we opened the picnic box to set out our paper plates, plastic forks and napkins. And then the Tupperware container of jerk chicken was lifted out of the box as though it were the highlight of the meal. Next came the pesto pasta salad and as the lid was gently lifted, I could smell the delicious combination of the herbs and garlic used to make the pesto sauce. And so filling my plate, I sat comfortably savouring my food and reminiscing about the evening past with my grandma in the kitchen making jerk chicken and pesto salad.

"First the chicken is dry basted with the spices and left to sit overnight soaking up the flavours of the rub. Knowing we were cooking this today, I made the chicken rub yesterday so it would be ready for roasting today," my grandmother informed me upon entering her kitchen the day before.

I often went to Grandma's house after school to say hi and have a snack with her. That day, we were prepared to make lunch for our Saturday beach trip and so I knew I'd be there a while longer as I learned another new recipe from her. The recipes she taught me were carefully guarded in a yellow bounded cookbook Grandma had in her possession since she was a teenager. The book had been given to her as a gift from an elderly rich lady who Grandma associated herself with by doing odd chores around her house earning a few pennies a day. While cleaning the house, Grandma had told me she would enter the lady's reading room and when no one was looking, she would memorize a recipe, taking it back with her to cook at home. The money she got from cleaning the older lady's home helped with buying the flour and ingredients used in the recipes. Grandma never knew she was being watched by the lady of the house who carefully stood just outside the room and admired the way Grandma took to that one book. The lady smiled each day as Grandma took time away from her duties to study another recipe and then carefully placed the book back on its shelf pretending she was dusting in and around the bindings of all the books on the bookcase. On the day Grandma left the older lady's home to attend nursing school, she was presented with the book as a gift and a parting present for all the time she had spent with the lady and for being as adoring and loving as a grandchild to this woman who had no children or grandchildren of her own.

"Take this with you, Dear," the older lady had told my grandmother. "You will need to nourish your own body as well as prepare healthy meals for the convalescents you will be tending to with your nursing job. This book has many healthy meals you can prepare with some simple ingredients common to the kitchen pantry. Remember me always through each meal you prepare and pray that God will heal all those who eat from your plate. Now, God speed, my child, and run along."

With that, my grandmother ran from the older lady's house with her arms wrapped around the book with such force that no one could have pried it from my grandmother's grasp. When Grandma told me this story for the first time, she had tears in her eyes and so I knew Grandma had to run from the lady's home so she wouldn't cry and make a fuss over leaving a woman who had so clearly become a great person in Grandma's heart. It's only this cookbook that Grandma has now of this lady's and she treasures each and every recipe from it ensuring she never forgets where it came from or how she received it.

I remember it clearly, page one hundred and one, had the recipe for jerk chicken and one day when I was looking through what was now an ancient cookbook, I had asked Grandma what jerk chicken was and why the chicken was a jerk, like how I heard the word used at school.

Grandma laughed at my words when I confused meanings and today was no different. I think I surprised her with my thoughts and if I could make Grandma laugh, then I was going to keep thinking and saying those things that brought her this reaction.

"The chicken is not a foolish jerk, Honey. Jerk is a way of making meat with strongly flavored spices, including hot peppers and a dry rub for grilling. We're going to grill this meat after it has marinated for a day with many spices rubbed over it for flavour. It's delicious served cold and makes for a great snack at the beach." And with that conversation, jerk chicken became the favourite lunch menu for our beach trips.

Today we're sprucing up a pasta salad with flavourful garlic and garden herbs by making a pesto paste to cover the homemade pasta. Grandma mixed the whole wheat flour, egg and water together to make the pasta dough and once it was rolled into a ball, she wrapped it in plastic allowing it to rest on the counter while she made the pesto paste.

"Emma, please peel this garlic and crush it with the side of the knife to break it open allowing the juices to flow out. Then place the garlic in this mixing bowl along with the crushed almonds, chopped parsley, olive oil, salt, pepper and grated cheese. Mix it on medium until the paste is smooth and well blended," Grandma instructed me.

While I made the pesto paste, Grandma went to the garden to fetch a few hot chili peppers, a ripe tomato, some chives, a head of lettuce, some tarragon, marjoram, savory, basil and thyme, all to add to the pasta salad. Grandma said the pesto paste was enough, but she liked the healing powers of the added herbs and so she looked for as many dishes to include them in as she could find. The jerk chicken and the pesto pasta salad were perfect recipes for adding many herbs and garden greens to.

Upon her return, she guided me on how to wash the fresh herbs and greens so the flavour wouldn't be lost and then set them aside on a towel for drying.

Making the pasta, she floured her breadboard, placed a small ball of dough on it and then began rolling it out with a wooden rolling pin. The rolling pin had handles on it that she held onto while the core rolled over the dough flattening it out to a smooth round shape. Once the dough was as thin as Grandma liked, she cut it into squares and then pinched each square in the center by hand to make a bow tie shaped noodle. Allowing this to sit for a while on the counter to dry, she prepared a pot of salted boiling water for the pasta to cook in.

"Only leave the noodles in the boiling water for a few minutes, just until they float," she coached me.

And so it was that I learned how to make pesto paste salad. The jerk chicken, she had seasoned the night before and so I didn't know which herbs and spices went into that until I read the recipe on page one hundred and one. Grandma placed the chicken on a baking sheet, put it into the oven and set the time for forty minutes. Once the pasta was cooked and cooled, she spread the pesto paste over the pasta, and then placed it in the refrigerator for our day at the beach tomorrow. Similarly, when the chicken was cooked, it too went in the fridge for safe keeping. And now, today, Grandma and I sit on the beach together on our blanket with plate in hand filled with jerk chicken and pesto pasta salad, filled with ingredients from Grandma's garden that are nutritious for our bodies.

"What did you bring for dessert Grandma?" I asked, not knowing what else she had packed in the picnic box.

"Chocolate chip peppermint cookies," she replied.

"With peppermint leaves from your own garden?" I probed.

"Yes, peppermint has a soothing effect on the digestive system and will help with digesting your food. It's also filled with chlorophyll for extra goodness. The dark chocolate is good for your heart and so I made you the best cookies I know how. Please help yourself to them, Emma, when you are ready."

Lunch was the best ever.

Jerk Chicken

Ingredients

4 large chicken legs with thighs attached
2 ground hot chili peppers or 1 tbsp dried cayenne pepper (to liking)
1 tsp black pepper
1 tsp salt
1tsp allspice
1 tsp turmeric
¼ cup oil (can be olive, sesame, almond, sunflower, canola, vegetable, grape

seed, peanut, etc)

Instructions

1. Wash chicken in cold water, pat dry and place in flat casserole dish.

2. Combine remainder of ingredients into a bowl to make a rub.

3. Spread rub onto chicken, cover with plastic wrap and store in refrigerator overnight.

4. Next Day, preheat oven to 400 degrees F. Remove chicken from casserole, place on broiler pan or a grilling cast iron pan.

5. Bake in over for 40-50 minutes or until chicken is thoroughly cooked to the bone.

6. Jerk chicken can also be cooked on low heat on the BBQ or broiled in the oven for the grilling effect. Ensure the chicken is thoroughly cooked before serving.

Pesto Pasta Salad

Pasta Recipe

Ingredients

2 cups whole wheat flour

1 cup cold water

2 eggs

3-5 lettuce leaves, chopped (optional)

1 tomato, chopped

¼ cup chopped fresh garden herbs to liking such as tarragon, marjoram, thyme, basil, chives, savory

Instructions

1. Combine flour, water and eggs in a food processor, dough mixer or large bowl by hand until a soft ball is formed and the dough is off the sides of the container.

2. More flour or water may have to be added to make the dough ball firm, yet soft, which occurs when it comes off the sides of the container-adjust as required.

3. Coat the dough ball with flour and wrap in plastic allowing time to rest for 30 minutes.

4. Remove dough ball from plastic, roll out using additional flour to keep from sticking to bread board.

5. Cut into desired shapes and set aside on floured cutting board, covering with a tea towel to keep fresh.

6. Cook pasta shapes in salted boiling water for 3 minutes or until pasta floats, then strain and rinse with cool water.

7. Lightly coat with oil to keep from sticking and place in fridge until chilled.

8. Add chopped lettuce leaves, and fresh chopped herbs. Add chopped tomato.

9. When pasta is chilled, mix in pesto paste to desired taste adding salt and pepper where required.

10. Pasta can be stored in refrigerator for up to 5 days. Left over uncooked pasta dough can be stored in refrigerator for up to three days.

Pesto Paste Recipe

Ingredients

5 large cloves of fresh garlic, peeled and crushed
¼ cup crushed nuts such as almonds, pine nuts or raw cashews
½ cup olive oil
1 medium bunch of fresh parsley, washed (can be basil, chard or spinach)
½ cup grated/crumbled cheese such as parmesan, romano, or feta cheese
Salt to taste -start with small amounts as this can be adjusted at the very end by stirring into mixture before storing

Instructions

1. Combine all ingredients in food processor and mulch until a smooth paste is created. For desired texture, add more oil, nuts or parsley as desired. Consistency should be that of softened butter.

2. Store in refrigerator for up to two weeks or freeze in ice cube trays and then transfer to plastic bag for longer term freezer storage.

Variation on Pesto Paste: Pesto Oil

Ingredients

5 large cloves of fresh garlic, peeled and crushed
½ cup olive oil
1 medium bunch of fresh parsley, washed (can be basil, chard, spinach or chives)
Salt to taste -start with small amounts as this can be adjusted at the very end by stirring into mixture before storing

Instructions

1. Combine all ingredients in food processor and mulch until a smooth paste is created. For desired texture, add more oil or parsley as desired. Consistency will be slightly liquid.

2. Store in refrigerator for up to one week or freeze in ice cube trays and then transfer to plastic bag for longer term freezer storage.

3. Add to any sauce, stew or directly to pasta, also tasty on potatoes.

6

CHARACTER

"On personal integrity hangs humanity's fate."
-- R. Buckminster Fuller

Grandma did not return to her nursing job after her family was born until much later in life when her children were grown. She didn't need to as Grandpa had worked as an engineer in the local steel plant for most of their married life, earning a good wage, enough to feed five children and pay the bills, keeping them in a modest lifestyle. They were both frugal with their money and kept costs as low as they reasonably could in the areas of utilities, groceries and in the products they bought. Grandma never paid for services she could perform herself like cleaning her house, laundering and sewing her clothes, and she cooked her meals from scratch growing most of her own food. With her vegetable and flower gardens and her hobby farm with chickens, pigs, rabbits and turkeys, Grandma always found a way to have delicious home cooked meals on the table. She bought the basics, the things she couldn't grow or make herself like flour, potatoes, rice or the items she needed to make articles from like cloth and soap. She set herself up to make her own final products like her meals, her clothes, her household accessories such as curtains and throw pillows and, she made her own cleaning and bathing products. And the best part about Grandma was that she loved doing it. She never felt deprived of anything and instead, turned it into positive thinking about how lucky she was to have the skills to do it all. Grandma could see the big picture in life and knew that what she was doing contributed to overall well being and that made her feel good.

"Feeling good is important to me, Emma," Grandma said. "Taking care of my own household keeps me fit, feeling like a young lady and I love being healthy," she continued. "I keep focused on being thankful for my God given talents and my good health. My own grandmother had a life much harder than mine. She had to build her home from the trees among her and she had horses to work her land where as I have a lawn tractor to help me out and electricity for power tools. My mom hand washed her family's clothes on a scrubbing board, whereas I have a machine to do it for me. First I had a ringer washing machine and then on the day I saw those new spinning washing machines for sale, I wanted to get one because I knew how hard it was to wash clothes from a scrub board down at the creek having done it many times alongside my mother. So I saved money by growing vegetables and selling them for a decent price and I looked around the yard for things to sell, things that I could recycle, and make use of again, and then I bought one of those ringer washing machines and years later, upgraded to the spinning type. Oh, I could have saved money from the house budget, but it seemed to me that having all this stuff around the house, just sitting here, was such a waste," she said as she waved her arms around the house indicating what she was talking about. "I felt a greater purpose to be kind to the land," she continued, "and salvage what was good before I lavishly spent money on items that would require space to keep. And so for the new items I bought, like the washing machine, I cleared out space by getting rid of the old items and that was how I got rid of most of the stuff your Uncle Sid collected during his days of depression when his family left him. Those washing machines saved me so much time and effort. No clothes drier for me though. I prefer to hang my clothes letting the fresh outside air blow through them, leaving them smelling fresh and crisp." And yet another way my grandmother was green.

"Today, Honey, we have automatic clothes washers, dryers, dish washers and heck, we even have a vacuum cleaner that just sucks up the dirt and takes it away. We don't have to sweep anymore, stirring up dust and dirt in the house filling our lungs with particles. The things you young folks have access to for cleaning up the house, and taking care of business these days makes your life way easier and yet, you don't time for anything or anyone, busy as you are, and doing what, I ask? Just what does everyone busy themselves with so much that they don't have time to sit with their friends and family anymore enjoying a meal together and talking about the things in life? Who knows how to cook anymore, much less grow a garden and harvest a crop? And who knows how to sew their own skirts and dresses much less fix a button that's popped off? A shame it is really. Little did our ancestors know that in trying to make a better life for our children and grandchildren we might have actually been doing them harm. Not much physical activity anymore or social engagements. In my day, we had dances every Friday night to go to and blow off steam and have some fun. These days, what do the kids who don't have money to be in organized sports do for fun and exercise? Get into trouble, that's what they do. They should be helping their families to care for their homes and taking pride in what they have instead of focusing on what they don't have, wanting to buy more and more, causing parents to work longer hours to pay for it all. And where does it all end up? In the dump, that's where. It's just not right and it makes for a society that doesn't contribute to its own well being. The concept of the community becomes defunct and neighbours stop knowing each other because they don't have time for each other, and when they stop knowing each other, they stop caring for each other too."

The things Grandma said made me think about our modern day conveniences and how some things were almost a given in every household whereas other things were the luxuries families competed for to get. Luxuries like better, higher grade washers with more options. So many options in fact, I almost expect the clothes to jump into the dryer from the washer themselves, or to fold themselves into neat piles so all I have to do is carry them upstairs and put them in my closet. And why are there bylaws that prohibit a close line in the yard that allows clothes to be dried naturally by the wind? What about cars? So many makes and models out there and they all have so many options. It's the way cars are financed today that seems to allow even the base model cars to have way too many gadgets in them knowing they won't possibly last long, but who really cared? The car owner wouldn't be keeping the car more than five years anyway and then the car ends up as scrap, filling the landfill sites. This seemed to be applying itself to home appliances too where they only lasted for five years and then had a major break down. What was the person who wanted to pay for a high quality item and keep it for twenty years going to do? Terrible really, and not good for the environment either with so much garbage going to the land fill sites.

I liked it when Grandma talked about the vacuum cleaner because in my own home, that one item was left in the middle of the floor all day and night long just like it was part of the furniture. I constantly turned it on giving the floors a quick once over in the heavy traffic areas like the side door, the kitchen and the entrance to the family room where the rug tended to catch the dirt from the bottom of everyone's socks as they entered the room to watch TV. Grandma didn't have a vacuum cleaner while she was raising her family and everyone wore their shoes on in the house making it virtually impossible to keep the hardwood floors clean. Rugs were something Grandma never had in her house as she said there was no reasonable way to clean them except for pounding the life out of them with a broom handle and that was too much work. Today, I luxuriate in the comfort and cleanliness of my rugs. I own a carpet cleaner and regularly, I wash the rugs because these small appliances make doing these things so easy. I have light beige carpets and my house is always bright and clean looking and yet I never use harsh chemicals to make it so. I'm thankful for my appliances, large and small because for everything my grandmother had to do by hand, I have an appliance to do it for me. Besides the obvious washer, dryer, dishwasher, vacuum cleaner, refrigerator, and stove, I have a food processor to cut up veggies, a blender to make smooth beverages with, and sauces and juices for my cooking. I even have a juicer for making liquid sauces like my favourite vegetable hot sauce, or my very own vegetable soup that tastes and looks like my favourite store bought canned soup but without the high cost or salt content of it and I know where my vegetables were grown and who has touched them. I can make soup whenever I want and add whatever ingredients I like. I don't have to look for a company that makes things the way I like it. And with canning and freezing available to me, I make larger batches on Sunday afternoons and store it away for a time when I want it on demand. I have so much flexibility now with the invention and availability of small and large appliances that I have no excuses for not make things at home. It's much cheaper too, which means I can spend less time finding ways to earn more money and spend more time with friends and family. I can do things my way and with less money. Wow, what a thought. The down side to all this is the high consumption of electricity used to run all these appliances. There was a man I once knew who tried to so something about this by generating his own electricity from the wind. He had an eighty foot tower in his front yard that on the very top of it, sat a small dc generator that used the motion from the wind to spin three long blades to create electricity. He gave tours of his windmill to the locals so one day I was able to see what he was doing and it was impressive too. There were large batteries in a room that were charged by the spinning windmill where electricity was stored for use in the house. There was a big box called an inverter that took the electricity from the batteries and changed it into the kind of power that the appliances could use, so he didn't have to pay the hydro company any money for their electricity. And then for heat, he had large solar windows in his living room and the daylight produced enough heat through those windows that it heated his whole house. It was sad when the old man died because no one else knew how to run that house except for him and so it was stripped down and sold for parts by the town. Grandma said he made green energy way before his time, and that the energy was green because it was clean and produced naturally without much waste and so before he died, she asked for his help to build her a water pumping windmill for her property enabling her to get the water up from the well without an electrical or gas powered pump. And so, that is how Grandma came to have a bit of green power on her property too.

Grandma loved to sew right into her old age because it kept her mind active reading about new ways to make fashions and new materials to use for changing up the look of dress. She could go from casual cotton and linen for around the house and neighbourhood, to silks and satins for out in the city. One time she even used spandex for the comfort of the gym on a pair of casual pants for me to wear to the office and this was before spandex became popular.

She was skilled at using light fabrics and heavy fabrics for different times of the year and she could add her own designs and measurements to fit my taste and body type when she made things for me. And all this was in her control.

Later in her aging years and after a day filled with activity, she spent her evenings watching TV in her sewing room staying in touch with her favourite programs. She bought an old wood stove looking electric fire place to heat the area making it cozy without the mess of wood. The electric 'wood stove' was so nostalgic she bought a second one for the kitchen joking, "If you can't handle the heat Emma, don't get out of the kitchen. Instead, just flip the switch to the heater off. The power will continue giving motion to the artistic flame and it will appear visually as though we have a beautiful fire going, but there won't be any heat coming from it."

I have it so easy compared to my family before me and with heightened awareness of their lifestyles, I can be very grateful for mine.

Money didn't come easy to Grandma or to her children although Grandpa did have a decent job until the steel factory closed. Working in the factory had been a hard job, but it was a huge disappointment to the community when it had been sold to a company overseas who merged it with yet another company and then transferred the business back to their home land leaving the local families with no further job opportunities and significantly reduced incomes. No one in the family married wealth, they just had enough money to get an education early enough in life and then to earn a modest living. Some earned diplomas, one or two earned degrees, some learned skilled trades, some had no education and some had no mentionable skill set, but the times didn't lend themselves to making lots of money, not like it was in years to come with the stock market increases and the influx of new people in the country through immigration. The industries in the Niagara region were the main livelihoods of the families and each family hoped their sons and grandsons would get jobs in the factories too, everyone that is, except my grandfather.

My grandfather was convinced that factories were for him and perhaps his sons, but not for his grandkids and so he tried to instill other skills in his family so they would be able to earn money in other professional areas. We didn't exactly meet his expectations, but none of us worked in factories either. The sad part is there are not many factories left for anyone to work in so it's not exactly by choice that none of us work in one. As they were in my grandfather's day, the factories are not in abundant and so money must be earned in other ways using different skill sets. At one time, there had been five or six factories in the area mostly making steel and steel products, but that mostly disappeared and much of what's left is old steel structures that have been abandoned or large plots of land that have been cleared of the industries. It will be interesting to see what becomes of the area and how the land that was once prosperous with jobs will be used in the future.

Grandma took what money she had from Grandpa's earnings and paid her bills and taxes first. After those were paid, she counted the amount left, decided what she could afford to buy for groceries and then bought the supplies she needed to make nutritious meals with. If there was money left over, Grandma decided what she would do with it. Her options were to save for a rainy day, buy extra fabric for future sewing projects or shop the sales for her food pantry. Grandma never wasted money. Never in my whole life did I see Grandma spend money on something she didn't need. But one day, I did see Grandma buy some gladiola seeds for her garden, which I thought was unusual because gladiolas couldn't be eaten.

"They're for selling, Emma," she explained. "In this way, I get to enjoy their beauty in my garden for the time they're growing and then they'll earn me money when I sell them. It's the best of both worlds."

I surprised Grandma with an unexpected visit one day, and when I entered her kitchen unannounced, I saw freshly picked yellow gladiolas placed in a vase on her table. Curious by this, I wondered what the special occasion was and when I called out to her by name she spun around from the stove so quickly she almost dropped her wood spoon to the floor. Dribbles of tomato sauce fell from the spoon onto her apron as she stood frozen in her spot looking at me.

"You have make-up on Grandma," I exclaimed, this being the first time I had ever seen Grandma dressed and made up so charmingly.

"Oh, well, yes, no, yes," she stumbled along.

"Grandma," I said slowly, "What's going on?"

"Nothing, dear Emma, now you just run along and we'll visit together this weekend when you're not in school. Go on home to do your homework, it's getting late." And with that, Grandma ushered me out the door. I'd find out what was going on somehow, but it was many years later when I did.

Several years later, I learned Grandpa had lost his job at the factory. Being so focused on my own life and naive when it happened, it hadn't occurred to me that Grandpa wasn't going to work anymore. When I did find out, I wondered if Grandma and Grandpa had money coming into the house to survive on and what I saw that day with the gladiolas on the table was Grandma preparing a dinner for a man who could provide her with a job. The job was at a nursing home for the elderly and the hiring process was competitive. Grandma's confidence in her nursing skills wasn't where it should have been as it had been a very long time since she had been in school, and so, Grandma had invited the head of the nursing home over for dinner without Grandpa knowing about it.

"I thought that if I could land the job, I could tell you about it later and that you wouldn't be mad about my going out to work," Grandma explained, attempting to keep Grandpa's ego from falling apart. "I wanted to get this job so money wouldn't be tight and I thought it was about time I put my schooling to use again and in ways other than raising a family. Don't get me wrong, I loved raising our family together each day and I so appreciated all you've done to provide for us, but things have changed, and now I can help too. Besides, I miss being a nurse."

And so it was over a warm and home cooked meal that Grandma interviewed for her job for which she received an offer of employment.

The nursing home had seen better days and was run down and inefficiently operated. The elderly folks within the walls were sickly and needed lots of attention but soon they began experiencing something unique to the elderly within the confines of this structure, thanks to Grandma's nurturing ability. This something was compassion, understanding and the longing to feel alive again.

"I was getting older and the lifestyles of the youth were getting younger," explained one occupant in the home to my grandmother. "You came here with your ways of the past, and began making us feel alive again," exclaimed another. "With you, came recipes from the old country, recipes that inspired my cooking as a young bride but have been long forgotten in this modern world and you brought stories with you that remind me of how happy I was once was. And your relationship with your granddaughter is one that I envy," a lady named Hannah exclaimed.

Hannah observed that I enjoyed visiting my grandmother after school while she worked evenings at the nursing home. It was always intriguing for me to look around the hallways and visit with the men and women in the lounge area.

Hannah continued her story, "I was from a Jewish community that was destroyed during the holocaust, and I knew so very little about my own parents and grandparents. My father is only a distant memory to me having been beaten up in the streets of Frankfurt in 1937, being left there to die, all alone. The family home in Germany had become Aryanised, meaning it had been taken over without compensation and given to a non-Jewish family and so my mother left Germany to work for a family in England as a domestic servant which meant she couldn't have a child with her and so it was then I was placed in a foster home and lived there until I answered a calling to become a volunteer nurse in a war hospital. It was in England that the spelling of my name was changed from the Hebrew spelling of Channah to the English spelling of Hannah, mostly because it was easier to adapt to the new spelling than it was to spell it out for so many."

Listening to this story while sitting by my grandmother's side, I heard Grandma gasp softly, as though she could feel the older woman's pain. My own grandmother had been a young married woman when the war was going on, but living in a very different country where peace and harmony existed. Canada was part of the Second World War, but the fighting occurred overseas and so the Canadians who had not been drafted were safe from the suffering and destruction that was happening a world away. There were those whose loved ones had been drafted to fight and lost their lives doing so. So many families had been disrupted during those times and their dreams crushed by the cold and cruel doings of war. Grandpa's job during the war had been as a young engineer working in the steel mill designing and producing quality steel for the weapons and planes and so Grandma and Grandpa and never been separated as this woman had been from her family.

"Grandma," I asked, "would you have risked yourself or your family to save somebody's life by hiding them in your own home, if they had come to you?"

"I don't know the answer to that, Emma, and I'm glad I didn't have to make that choice. I do know that I would have opened my home to foster children of the war had I been asked, but I wasn't called to do that," she replied deep in thought.

Hannah's story ended happily as she married Jack, an American gentleman on leave from the war three years later and raised a family together in America before coming to Canada with their daughters. Hannah and Grandma turned the nursing home on its heels by learning to dance the waltz and by creating beautifully crafted meals in the nursing home's kitchen, sharing recipes. Through example, they reinforced in the other residents the basics of human empathy and understanding for each other by tolerating and respecting the differences, and in caring for one another as a community.

Hannah's best shared recipe was for challah, a yeast leavened Jewish bread twisted into braids and prepared specially for the Sabbath.

Challah

Ingredients

2 cups warm water
2 tbsp dry active yeast
7 cups unbleached flour
1 tbsp salt
1/2 cup sugar
1 egg
1/2 cup oil, sunflower or canola
Poppy or sesame seeds (optional)

Instructions

1. Beat an egg to be used as the Glaze in Step 12.
2. Dissolve yeast in 1 tbsp sugar and warm water, allowing to sit for 10-15 minutes.
3. Add remaining sugar, salt & 5 cups flour. Mix well.
4. Add egg and oil and remaining 2 cups of flour and continue mixing.
5. When the dough pulls away from the sides of the bowl, transfer it to a floured breadboard and hand knead it for 10 minutes or until dough is

smooth & elastic, springing back when pressed lightly.

6. Oil all sides of the dough and place in an oiled bowl.

7. Cover with a damp towel & let rise in a warm place for 2 hours, punching down every 15 minutes. After 2 hours, don't punch down but instead, place dough back on breadboard.

8. Split into 3 equal portions and roll each piece and shape into 3 braided sections to form one loaf.

9. Place loaf on parchment paper and move to baking stone.

10. Allow challah to rise for another 1/2 an hour.

11. Preheat oven to 375°F.

12. After the challah has risen glaze it with the beaten egg & top with poppy or sesame seeds.

13. Bake for 25 minutes.

14. Turn oven off & leave challah in oven for another 10 minutes (Grandma used this technique with all her bread).

15. Remove from oven and place on cooling rack.

7

BUTTER AND CHOLESTEROL

"You are the butter to my bread, and the breath to my life"
-- Julia Child

Making butter with Grandma was fun. She always bought the heavy cream from a favourite farmer and then churned it all by herself in her homemade churner until the cream became butter. Grandma invented whipped butter and soft butters by adding liquid sunflower oil to her freshly churned butter making it creamy, smooth and soft. Sometimes it got too soft and was liquid but once Grandma got her fridge, this was never a problem. She intentionally made it soft so it was easy to spread on her homemade breads.

"It's healthy, she insisted, "much healthier than using those hydrogenated spreads sold in the markets. Those spreads are made with chemicals, keeping butter soft, and will be the harm of us one day," Grandma insisted.

Grandma concerned herself with the manufacturing processes of food that became rampant in the decades and became quite frustrated with friends and family who began consuming those food products in large quantities abandoning the ways of the families before them, those who made real food from whole ingredients. It was the chemicals found in processed foods that Grandma despised the most and when she shopped she looked for whole foods, bypassing food products on the shelves.

"Food products," she exclaimed, "are confusing to people because they look delicious and yet they're usually so refined and processed, containing so many chemicals that the body has no way of using the ingredients found in them for building and repairing or for supporting our immune systems. And yet, the marketing campaigns behind those products can be so convincing, they compel us to buy. We can get sick eating these food products in such large quantities, storing the chemicals they contain in our cells and organs; overloading them to the point where they can't do the job they were made to do anymore."

And so Grandma stuck to her principles of enjoying her cooking, her gardens and her whole food recipes and I have to say, she did enjoy good health until the day she quietly died of old age.

"Eat butter", Grandma told me when I toasted bread. "It's real food and has healthy oil when mixed with sunflower or olive oil and whipped as butter. Your body has to have some of its calories each day from good fat or you'll suffer with ailments such as high cholesterol and possibly arthritis. When you eat good oils, your body will get its energy needed for the day and will use it to lubricate your joints, skin and hair. It's like having oil in the car. It's needed to make the car run and without it, the car engine will seize."

Grandma knew just enough about so many things that she could relate them to each other and so her stories had meaning to everyone. If the farmer talked about his tractor, then Grandma told stories about farming. If the grocery clerk talked about cash registers and the price of food, Grandma related them to house hold finances and grocery budgets and if the doctor talked about the body, Grandma related it to machines, food and flowing rivers, as she referred to the fluids in her body. She had a knack for communicating and relating to almost everyone and her nursing background gave her the knowledge she needed for good nutrition and healthy lifestyles.

"In the newspaper today, I read about this substance in our blood called cholesterol and it's both good and bad for you," Grandma explained to me while I watched her this particular morning churning butter hoping she'd make some chocolate chip cookies with it later. "I don't quite understand what that means. Something was mentioned about the body making it's own cholesterol which is a good thing and then there's the cholesterol that we eat in food that can be both good and bad depending on what kind of cholesterol it is. Letters LDL and HDL are used to name the cholesterol but not much was said about what each is, only that LDL is harmful and HDL is good cholesterol. What I don't know is which foods it's found in."

"Will my skin and hair be shiny if I eat good cholesterol, Grandma?" I asked.

"There's a good question," she thoughtfully replied. "I think it's the fat that makes your skin and hair shiny, and not the cholesterol. I don't know what the cholesterol does except that it's there and as I said, the body makes it own, enough so none has to be consumed. It's in food and in the body too. I'll have to do more reading to know for sure and next time I see the doctor, I'll ask."

"Why is the cholesterol bad?" I probed for more information thinking I didn't want any bad stuff in my body.

"The doctor who wrote the article said it scars arteries and forms a hard substance and then the blood can't flow through the veins. He said it was something like when the water pipes in the house get dirty on the inside and the water can't come out the taps. That's never happened to me so I think it's easier to think about what happens when the drain pipes get plugged and the water won't go to the sewer but instead, stays backed up in the sink. The plunger can force the clog down, but the doctor said we don't want to force any blood clots through our veins because this can cause strokes and heart attacks when the blood clot moves and lodges somewhere else in our bodies. It's very complicated but the basics are like this; we have to eat the right kinds of fat and cholesterol so our bodies are nourished. We don't want to treat our organs like garbage cans dumping all the bad stuff into them, because unlike the trash, we can't just take the clogged stuff in our bodies out to the trash every week. No, we have to live with it and hope our body can clean itself. Lemon, I hear, is a really good body cleaner and the liver especially likes to be cleaned with lemon. Drinking a cup of water, either hot or cold, with lemon in it every morning is supposed to be really good for this."

To this day, my favourite beverage in the hot summer months is combining a fresh piece of lemon with cucumber and water with ice in a blender and drinking this before going to work or drinking it after a hot day of playing golf or mountain biking or working in the gardens. I find this drink to be so refreshing and hydrating that my skin positively glows after drinking this mixture for just a couple of days in a row. Grandma told me it's because the lemon is cleaning my liver and when I have a clean liver my skin will show healthy and clear. This must be true, because I often get compliments from people on the clarity of my skin commenting on how young I look, yet I'm in my forty's. I remember those days when Grandma told me about cholesterol and clean organs and blood, and I try to incorporate her teachings into my menu planning for my own family. Cucumbers, I've learned since, have vitamins A, B1, B6, C, D, folic acid, calcium, magnesium and potassium and are considered as being an energizing food. They contain silica and sulfur which promotes and stimulates hair growth, healthy joints and strong connective tissues and they're good for all soft tissue, including lungs.

Whipped Butter

Ingredients

1 cup of butter, softened
1 cup of Oil (Canola, sunflower, almond, grape seed, mild tasting olive)
Salt (optional)

Instructions

1. Combine ingredients in food processor with the interior blade for whipping starting with the softened butter and slowly adding the oil for desired consistency.
2. Add salt to taste.
3. With a rubber spatula, transfer butter to an air tight container and store in refrigerator for use. This whipped butter will be soft and spreadable right from the refrigerator.

Almond Butter

Ingredients

1 cup of almonds, can be any quantity
½ cup of almond oil
Several tablespoons of water

Ingredients

1. Place almonds in food processor and whip until fine, adding the oil and water in small quantities until desired consistency is achieved. Note, this may take several minutes to finely smoothen out the almonds. This is a personal preference, so taste and test along the way.
2. Transfer almond butter to an air tight container and store in the

refrigerator for use.

Butter Variation:

a. This technique can be used for any nut including peanuts and cashews.

b. Try flavouring it up using different oils such a grape seed, canola, sunflower oil, flax seed oil.

c. Add fruit instead of water, such as blueberries, strawberries, peaches, grapes, etc.

d. Honey can be added to any whipped nut butter for extra flavour and antioxidants.

Cucumber Lemon blender beverage

This is a refreshing beverage for hot days, revitalizing the skin, hydrating the body, adding moisture to soft tissues such as ligaments, lung, and sinuses and for cleansing the liver.

Ingredients

1 English cucumber, well washed, but not peeled
¼ fresh lemon, washed and seeds removed (lemon juice can be used as a substitute)
1-1½ cups of water
4 or 5 ice cubes

Instructions

1. Cut cucumber and lemon into chucks fitting into blender.

2. Add enough water to cover the top of the cucumber/lemon chunks.

3. Add ice cubes.

4. Blend until smooth, and pour into cups. This beverage is best consumed through a straw to keep it well mixed in the glass so all the flavours are tasted together.

8

CHRISTMAS COOKIES

"A balanced diet is a cookie in each hand." -- Author Unknown

Tomorrow is the first day in December and the Christmas toy drives are out in full force including the one where I work. No one volunteering here earned much money at their jobs, but somehow we all seemed to gather around donating what we could, providing those much less fortunate than ourselves with the chance to experience the true meaning of life in a world that is filled with love and care.

"It's in giving that we receive," my grandmother repeated time and again the well known phrase.

So today, I give again. What I really wanted to do was to see the person who I was giving this gift to. I wanted to experience their emotion and in that way, I would feel it too. I thought about the recent article in the headlines that honoured one of our police officers for buying a man a pair of winter boots, a homeless man who had only bare feet. The sincere moving part about the story was that not only did this wonderful human being purchase a pair of warm boots, socks and mitts for this man, but he also kneeled down to help him don them. Tears of compassion came to my eyes when I envisioned him doing this.

Remembering back to past Christmases, I thought of the years my classmates and I shared baked goods with each other and one year, in particular, came to mind. It was the year I learned to bake Christmas cookies.

"Oh, you have no excuse. If you have time to talk and play with your friends and watch TV, then you have time to bake your own cookies.' My grandma always had a point to make and this time was no different. I had come into her kitchen asking her if she had a bag of store bought cookies that I could take outside to share with my friends.

"Fifteen minutes, that's all it takes," she carried on.

"In your recipe, you'll have wholesome ingredients that will help make you strong and healthy. Only you with your cleanly washed hands and your clean utensils will have touched your food. You can share the fruits of your labour with your friends knowing you're giving them a healthier snack because all the ingredients will come from the pantry and not the chemical factory. Come Dear, let's spend some time together. I'll show you how to make the most delicious cookies that will make you popular at school and in the play ground."

I looked up at Grandma and saw her smile. Her eyes were bright with a twinkle and her cheeks positively glowed. It was at this moment I realized my grandma was a very beautiful woman with her brown hair, green eyes and well defined cheekbones. I couldn't help wondering if I would ever be as beautiful as she is right now.

"Grandma, what are cookies made of?" I asked.

"Well, let's just see." My grandmother liked to think about her answer before speaking out. "I have a recipe here that my mom used when she and I made them together, a time when I was a little girl wanting a bed time snack. We also made these cookies together every Christmas. We'll use some whole wheat flour, sugar, eggs, sunflower oil, some butter, and some chocolate chips."

"Can I break the egg?" Standing beside my grandma was the greatest feeling in the world. I could smell her lavender scent and feel the warmth from her body. From this warmth emanated love and comfort, and I feared the day she would be gone. God, please let my grandma live forever," I whispered so she couldn't hear me.

"What's that, Dear?"

"Can I break the egg?"

Grandma had a special way of breaking eggs so no shells ever got into the recipe. Crack! I smacked the egg on the side of a clean bowl and then quickly began moving the slippery white part from the shells by grabbing the yolk in the hub of the empty shell and passing it back and forth from one half of the shell into the other all the while watching the white part fall into the bowl below.

"Oh, a piece of shell fell in with the white part. I'll get it out Grandma, using this wood spoon. You never spill egg shells in because you're really good at it," I said while digging in with the spoon removing the one piece of shell that fell in.

"Emma, why did you separate the white from the yolk?"

"Because I like to play with it. I love how the white sticks together and moves like a glob." At that, my grandma arched her back, lifted her head high and laughed a good hearty laugh with such humour, I began laughing with her. And there we stood, at her kitchen counter, laughing and sharing a 'together' moment as Grandma warmed some milk on the stove to go with the cookies. Those were the best cookies I ever ate.

"Teacher," Emma spoke out in class next day, "do you want one of the cookies I made last night at my grandma's?"

Teacher, as I liked to call her, went to the front of the class and announced, "I have here a cookie made by Emma and her grandmother. Made with their own hands," she emphasized. When she said this, she showed them her hands, palms upward, and then placed the cookie in the center of her left palm.

Teacher did many things that showed the talents of her students that were not taught in class. She always believed we were gifted and wanted us to share these gifts.

"Do you have more cookies, Emma? Enough to share with the class?" And with that, I pulled out my school bag where my grandma placed the nicely wrapped treats and passed them around.

After handing them out, Teacher asked, "Children, have you had enough to eat now?" And the class responded that they did. When we had finished the snack the class turned their attention to the reading assignment, but I sat day dreaming of the night before, imagining my grandmother laughing and sharing her time with me.

__Chocolate Chip Cookies__

Ingredients

1 cup of softened butter
½ cup white sugar
1 cup brown sugar
2 eggs
2 ½ cups whole wheat or unbleached white flour
1 tbsp sunflower oil
1 tsp baking soda
1tsp salt
1 tbsp pure vanilla extract
2 cups of dark or milk chocolate chips

Instructions

1. Preheat oven to 340 degrees Fahrenheit.

2. Mix all ingredients except the chocolate chips together in a mixing bowl and using either a hand held mixer or a mixing machine, mix until well blended. Then stir in chocolate chips.

3. Spoon 1 inch size balls of cookie dough onto a non-stick cookie sheet or line tray with parchment paper and lightly press each dough patch with a fork to flatten to desired thickness (Grandma liked to leave the cookies thick and so she only lightly tapped them with a fork).

4. Bake 8-10 minutes until lightly brown and immediately remove from oven and place each cookie on a cooling rack using a spatula. All to cool before eating. Cookies will be soft and chewy.

Variation:

To make mint cookies:

a. Use mint chocolate chips or

b. Use fresh pepper leaves from the garden or

c. Use pure peppermint extract instead of vanilla

Gingerbread Cookies

Ingredients

1 cup butter
½ white sugar
½ cup brown sugar
2 eggs
2 ½ cups whole wheat or unbleached flour
½ cup molasses
1 tsp baking soda
1 tsp pure vanilla extract
1 tbsp ground cinnamon

½ tbsp ground cloves

½ tbsp ground ginger

½ tsp salt

Instructions

1. Preheat oven to 340 degrees Fahrenheit.

2. Mix all ingredients together in a bowl using a hand held mixer and then a wooden spoon or a mixing machine. This dough will be thick and so a bread hook may have to be used when using a mixing machine.

3. When dough is mixed, roll parts of the batter out using a rolling pin and parchment paper. Note that if the dough is too gooey, then let wrap in plastic and place in frig for half an hour before rolling.

4. Cut cookies with a gingerbread man cookie cutter and place each cookie on a tray lined with parchment paper.

5. Bake for 10 minutes until done and place on cooling rack before serving.

Cookies and Pudding

Vanilla Pudding

Ingredients

2 cups whole or 2% milk

½ cup cornstarch

½ cup sugar

¼ tsp salt

3 tbsp pure vanilla extract

Instructions

1. In a medium sized pot on the stove, combine all ingredients except vanilla and whisk together over medium heat.

2. When milk mixture begins to warm, use a wooden spoon to constantly

stir and reduce heat to low. Allow mixture to heat and thicken while stirring constantly. This takes about 20 minutes.

3. When thick, remove from heat and stir in vanilla.

4. Pour into a mixing bowl. Allow to cool before placing in frig overnight.

5. Using your favourite cookie recipe, make cookies and set aside.

6. Next day, whip the pudding mixture in the mixing bowl using a hand held mixer until smooth and creamy. Place pudding back in refrigerator for an hour to continue chilling before serving with cookies. Cookies can be crumpled into a serving dish and topped with pudding or dipped directly into pudding and eaten whole.

9

CABBAGE ROLLS

"An idealist is one who, on noticing that a rose smells better than a cabbage, concludes that it makes a better soup." -- *H.L. Mencken*

For comfort food, Grandma made cabbage rolls. Pataha, also known as pierogies, and cabbage rolls, were both served at every Christmas Eve dinner when the whole family came to Grandma's house to celebrate the birth of Christ. After decorating the Christmas tree and drinking the traditional eggnog, she served the family her traditional dinner of cabbage rolls and pierogies.

"Cabbage makes a delicious soup, Emma," my cousin, Chris, said matter of fact, one Christmas Eve while we were decorating the tree together. Grandma had given us our own section to place ornaments on as we saw fit to hang.

"What?" I asked nonchalantly, all the while holding up and examining a delicate ceramic gingerbread house ornament, not having really heard what Chris had said.

"Cabbage makes a delicious soup," she repeated.

"So what?" I offered up to the conversation, "when have you had cabbage soup?"

"Never, but I read about it. I read that in Europe, people make cabbage soup all the time because cabbage is nutritious and inexpensive and if they eat it all the time, it must be a delicious soup. I know you like to talk about cooking and so I thought you might have known about cabbage soup," she went on to explain. Intrigued by her desire to engage me in conversation, I hung the ornament I was holding on the tree branch by its red ribbon and then I told her how Grandma and I had prepared the Christmas Eve dinner together.

"Using large leaves from the cabbage, we carefully filled each one with ground beef, pork, onions and just a bit of rice," I began my rendition.

"Never use too much rice, Emma, otherwise people won't like to eat your cabbage rolls. Fill them with meat and onions and just a showing of rice for the look of white flecks, and in this way, there will be meat protein, vegetables and starches from all the ingredients to give everyone a healthy and satisfying meal. You'll have them eating all night long whilst they laugh together and reminisce about their younger years and all their past Christmases together."

Sprinkling in freshly ground beef, salt, pepper, thyme, onions, and adding long grain rice that had been previously cooked to the raw ground beef and pork, and using bright green cabbage leaves, Grandma and I spent two hours rolling cabbage rolls a month before Christmas. Once they were rolled, she covered them with her canned tomato juice and froze them so they would be ready for her on Christmas Eve morning when she would place them in the oven on a very low heat to simmer all day waiting for the hungry guests to gobble them up. In earlier years, Grandma made them only a day or two before Christmas so they were fresh but as she grew older she bought a freezer and started making her Christmas food ahead of time making her days leading into Christmas much easier for herself. She never stopped making cabbage rolls or pataha for her family no matter how easy it was to buy them. Her food had to be made with loving hands and for her, this was her gift to all of us. I think it was the best gift she could have given me because not only did I get homemade cabbage rolls and pataha every Christmas, I also received the gift of the recipe and so now I can make them too. Teaching me her home making skills was the greatest gift Grandma gave me and for that, I am thankful.

What I like so much about this homemade food is that it comes with so little packaging, very little handling by other people and it's inexpensive compared to buying food that someone else has made. And I can put as much or as little of each ingredient in as I want. I can use ground beef, pork, chicken, turkey or tofu. I can also add variety to my meals with little expense, and the effort I apply to making this food is energy well spent. Like my grandmother, I cook with love and joy and my days are brightened by the contribution to healthy living I make with each meal. Similar to the cabbage rolls, the pierogies too, were sometimes made and cooked prior to the holidays and then frozen, individually at first, then together in a freezer bag, waiting for Christmas Eve when Grandma placed the frozen, cooked pierogies into a baking dish then layered them with simmered onions. She chopped the onions, softly simmered them in a pan with oil, salt and pepper and when the onions were a clear, translucent colour, she evenly spread them over the frozen pierogies in the baking dish. She then covered the dish with either its own lid or some foil, whichever she had available to her.

She first placed the baking dish with the cabbage rolls into the oven for the first hour to get them started because they took longer to heat up in the middle than the pierogies did. When those were near done, she then placed the second casserole dish containing the pierogies and onions into the oven alongside the cabbage rolls and adjusted the oven temperature to just below boiling, which was 200 degrees Fahrenheit. The pierogies slowly defrosted and warmed up, staying in the oven for several hours until we were ready to eat. Grandma set the dinner time based on how well the decorating was going. She checked on the food ensuring it was hot, and if not quite where she wanted it to be in terms of temperature, she turned up the oven to speed things along. Nothing was ever burnt because she was careful to watch it as it heated.

Delicious smells warmed the house all afternoon while we decorated the tree and the house and drank eggnog, sometimes with rum. Decorating the tree was a special time in Grandma's house. She took such great care ensuring all the decorations were carefully hung and if needed the crystal bulbs were polished. Grandma had special bulbs for special people in her life, both passed away and present. Some bulbs were from childhood memories and some had been gifts commemorating special events in people's lives such as first home, first Christmas together, favourite pets and some were plain bulbs intended to stand the test of time. One particular ornament was a small string woven doll that Grandma had received as a gift from her mother when she was only six years old. As each special ornament was hung, Grandma spoke fondly of the people and of the times surrounding the event and I could often see tears welling up in her eyes as she spoke. I softly said a prayer for her as she bravely told each story. In the background there played soft Christmas carols and along with the smells from the oven, the rum and eggnog effect taking place, and the peaceful gentleness with which the tree was decorated, I fell into love with Christmas.

After the hearty meal, the family exchanged their modest gifts as they did every year and we all treasured Christmas Eve at Grandma's house for another year as we were to do for her entire life.

"Some of you will carry on the tradition for your own families come the day when I am no longer here," lamented Grandma one cold and snowy Christmas Eve. The thought of that sent chills up my spine.

"Grandma," I asked, changing the subject, "what's in cabbage?"

I knew Grandma loved it when I asked her about the food and what was in it that makes it healthy for people to eat. And I knew I had to change the subject quickly as I was beginning to cry thinking there might come a day when Grandma wouldn't be with us. And so, with a smiling face, Grandma charmed us with her story of how cabbage is grown and how it contains all kinds of nutrients having tremendous health benefits.

Cabbage Rolls

Ingredients

1 large green cabbage
2 medium onions, sautéed
1 cup long grain rice, steamed
4 tomatoes, blended into liquid in food processor or blender
Salt & Pepper to taste
1tbsp ground thyme
1 lb ground beef, pork, chicken or turkey or tofu if desired

Instructions

1. In a large pot of boiling water, carefully place cabbage to boil, steaming the leaves off the cabbage and removing them as they loosen from the head. Place leaves aside to cool. If it's too difficult to remove the leaves while steaming the cabbage, then leave in pot to boil for about 20 minutes. Allow to cool before removing cabbage from pot. This can be done several hours ahead of time or the day before making cabbage rolls.

2. In a bowl, combine ground meat, sautéed onions, steamed rice and salt

and pepper. Mix thoroughly.

3. Taking each leaf from the cabbage head, roll a ball of meat mixture from the bowl into the leaf. Place each roll into a casserole.

4. When casserole is filled, pour tomatoes over the cabbage rolls, being careful not to overfill as this will boil over in the oven. Note: cabbage rolls can be cooked in a slow cooker or oven.

5. Set in oven, covered, at 350 degrees Fahrenheit for 1 hour or until fully cooked, being careful to not overflow the casserole.

6. Serve warm or cold. Topping each roll with sour cream and/or ketchup is a popular way of serving.

Variation:

a. Using the above meat mixture, stuff cleaned out green and red bell peppers and add meat mixture to the inside of each pepper. Cook similarly to cabbage rolls in a tomato juice.

b. Add basil, and or oregano for additional seasonings.

Pierogies, also known as Pataha

Ingredients

Dough

1 egg
1 tbsp salt
1 cup of flour
1/8 cup cool water

Potato and Cheese Filling

2 large potatoes, peeled
½ cup grated cheddar cheese (or your favourite cheese)
2-3 tbsp butter
Salt and Pepper as desired (about 1 tbsp of salt and ½ tbsp pepper)

1 medium sautéed onion (optional to add on top while serving)
3 slices cooked bacon (optional to add on top while serving)
Sour cream (optional)

Instructions

1. Mix egg, salt, flour, and water into a dough and allow the dough ball to rest for 30 minutes covered under a tea towel or wrapped in plastic wrap to keep fresh.

2. While dough is resting, boil 2 large peeled potatoes and mash together with grated cheddar cheese. Do not add any liquid such as milk or water to mashed potatoes. These can be prepared a day ahead.

3. Salt and Pepper the potatoes to taste and allow to cool.

4. While the mashed potatoes are cooling, roll out the dough into thin slices, and cutting it into circles by using the rim of a wide mouthed glass or canning jar lid.

5. Place mashed potatoes into one half of the round dough, not too close to the edge, and flip the other half of the dough over the potatoes so the ends of the dough meet.

6. Using a fork, press down on the dough edges to seal. Place on floured cutting board until ready to cook.

7. Once all the pierogies are prepared, boil a large pot of water on the stove.

8. Place pierogies in boiling water to cook for about 3 minutes, just until they float.

9. Removing the pierogies from the boiling water can be tricky so be sure to have a spoon with holes, a large colander and a bowl underneath the colander ready to catch the dripping hot water.

10. Spoon each pierogi into the colander to drain and then pour into a clean bowl, adding butter to keep pierogies from sticking to each other.

11. Enjoy hot or cold, and served with sour cream or Greek yogurt if desired. Adding black pepper on top is a delicious way to eat pierogies (pataha). Simmered onions and/or bacon can be added on top of the cooked pierogies for enhanced flavour.

10

WORK PLACE DAY OF MOURNING

"Your sudden death has touched our lives and hearts. The way you have inspired us has touched us even more." -- Author Unknown

Today would have been my father's birthday. He was born April 28 and died 69 years later, just two months before his 70th birthday. These are the kind of dates a person never forgets. At work, International Day of Mourning is a scheduled event every April 28th remembering co-workers, friends and family who have lost their lives on the job and reflecting on the past to build a safer future. During the minute of silence, tears fill my eyes and my throat chokes. I don't share my pain with anyone around me while I remember my own father who died from asbestos poisoning he received in his work place. I think about the hazards in the company I work at, including the asbestos that is known to exist. I ask God to comfort me and pray for a gentle death like my father had but one that's from very old age and not a work related injury or illness.

My father died peacefully in his sleep and escaped the severe pain and suffering of a horrible lung disease that was about to get worse. The diagnosis of his death was heart failure caused by his lung disease and yet he was spared the agony of being on oxygen tanks with tubes in his nose and having to take strong pain medication. The vision I will have of my father will always be that of a healthy man who was vibrant, strong and full of energy. But unfortunately, a vision, a memory is all there is. It's purely sad he has no headstone on his plot of land in the graveyard. Without it, never will his descendants know of his life here on earth or have a place in this world that marks his existence. There's no place for me to take my children to pray over their grandfather. It's like he never existed and the children have been robbed of him. Oh, the family tried to have the headstone placed down, but the cold at heart remained unchanged.

Many people tell me I'm just like my father, and each time I hear that, I think what a blessing it is to be so much like a man who was inspiring, inventive, hard working and generous. He loved to laugh, dance, build homes, repair things, hunt, fish, and he loved to help people. He had a gift of seeing ways out of problems that others just couldn't see. He saw ways of making people's lives easier through short term but hard work that reaped rewards in the end. And he loved to eat! Not just any food, but really good food.

My father helped inspire my cooking skills by being particular on how he liked his food and by encouraging me to experiment with new ingredients in my cooking, such as wild game and fish. The cooking time, seasoning, texture and quality of every meal were critiqued by him and when he gave his approval, it was like winning a million dollars. The elation would stay with me for days inspiring more creations, paying attention to the details and working my magic on the next meal. He loved variety in his meals and so they ranged from Italian to Ukrainian to Hungarian to Canadian inspired cuisine.

I call earthy foods such as potatoes, carrots, onions, wheat and wild game Canadian food but know we don't have exclusivity on any of it. Food was brought to Canada by our ancestors, but the various Canadian climates allow for so much food to be grown and most of it right here in Ontario. My own father was an avid hunter and fisher and remained so right until his passing, bringing me venison from his most recent hunts and fish from the lakes of Ontario. I always looked forward to those visits and he elated in giving me the food knowing I would thoroughly enjoy it, like he did. He boasted about the quality of the meat and the fact that there were no hormones injected into the animals. If the lake became polluted, my dad stopped fishing there. It was also through my father's teachings that I learned some foods had chemicals and additives in them and this sparked me to read articles about the health of farm animals and the meat sold in grocery stores. Living near the countryside, I was able to talk to farmers and from them, I learned that some commercial grade meat did indeed have growth hormones and antibiotics in them in some countries and areas. I learned it was good to know where the meat came from and then I could determine the quality of the meat. And so I began a life long journey of making it my business to know and understand what was in the food I ate. He and Grandma shared a passion for food and passed it on to me.

"Grandma, can we make lamb stew for supper? I just love lambs."

Grandma was standing in the kitchen with her red apron tied around her waste stirring a big pot of something on the stove. She had just started making it so I couldn't tell from the smell what it was it.

"Now how does my little six-year old know she loves lamb stew?" Grandma asked.

"Lyle down the street, Grandma, he knows all about baby lambs because he has lots of them. He showed me the lambs and we played with them in the field. They were white with really soft fur and little pink ears and cute black noses. He said these lambs were going to have thick wool and would be very warm come the winter time. And then he fed them and I asked what that sloppy stuff was that was going into their feed dishes and he said it was lamb stew. It looked really good too, kind of like porridge, but Lyle, he wouldn't let me touch none of it so I couldn't have a taste. I told him I was gonna ask my grandma to make me some lamb stew cause she's the best cook in the whole world and I knew she'd know how to make lamb stew. Do ya, Grandma? Do ya know how to make lamb stew?"

The smile coming from my grandmother's face was so genuinely beautiful that I forgot all about what I asked her for and instead returned the gigantic hug she was giving me. She told me we were having potato leek soup for dinner because that was what she was already making and that I should run along now Dear, and wash up for dinner in about an hour.

It wasn't until much later in life that I understood the meaning behind that smile and the hug that went with it that day. It was so like her to not upset me with hard reality and cold facts allowing me to remain youthful and innocent for as long as the world would let me be. I love you, Grandma.

After I had washed up, I returned to the kitchen and watched as Grandma made the potato leek soup and saw her scrubbing the remaining potatoes with a scouring pad to remove all the dirt and eyes on the skin. For this soup, she left the skins on the potatoes because these were early summer potatoes, freshly grown and new from her garden and the skins were light in colour and filled with nutrients. These potatoes have yellowish skins and white flesh.

"What's in a potato, Grandma," I asked?

"You're so inquisitive, Emma, I think you ought to consider a job in the food industry," she commented, but went on to explain the potato to me. "The potato has a starchy flesh on the inside and tastes great with any meat dish as the flesh on the inside is creamy and quite filling so you'll feel full after eating them. The skins have fibre, potassium, vitamins B6 and C and niacin. When grown in good quality soil, silica is present and silica is good for strong hair, nails and joints. See here, Emma, look at the starch in the potato when I cut into it." Slicing the knife through the raw potato, I could see the white starchy liquid ooze out and I tasted it by putting some on my finger. It tasted awful, but Grandma said it would taste better once it was cooked.

She finished washing the last few potatoes then cut them into cubes, rinsed them off and placed them in the pot on the stove that she had filled with enough water to cover the tops of the potatoes. Grandma then cut into slices a bunch of leeks that she had pulled out of a bowl of water in the refrigerator and placed those in the same pot with the potatoes. She added some salt, as Grandma said, 'to taste'. She then covered the pot with a lid and left it on the stove to simmer for the next hour. Tonight's dinner was going to be potato leek soup with toast and butter.

As we ate dinner together, Grandma carefully pointed out the nutrients in the ingredients she added to the soup, repeating herself about the potatoes but adding new information such as the goodness of leeks.

"Leeks are in the onion and garlic family, Emma, and first came from Central Asia. According to my own mother, Europeans loved them and harvested them for centuries before they came over to North America where they can grow in colder climates. They have iron, manganese, folic acid, and vitamin C which can support the immune system helping to fight off colds. Leeks are mainly harvested in the fall and so are here just in time for the common cold season when we can make these delicious soups to stay healthy with, and they come out when the potatoes are ready to dig up too which make them perfect compliments to each other. Today, we are using leeks that I dehydrated last fall and stored in the cold cellar. I rehydrated them in some water yesterday knowing I was going to cook this soup today. In the fall time, we will use fresh leeks from the garden for our soup when they are finished growing.

Potato Leek soup

Ingredients

6 medium potatoes
1 bunch fresh leeks
4 tblsp olive oil
4 cups of water
1 cup whole milk (or any other milk or cream)
Salt and Pepper (to taste)

Instructions

1. Wash the potatoes and remove any eyes. If the potatoes are new, leave the skins on, else peel them.
2. Cut into bite sized cubes and rinse with cold water before placing in a medium sized cooking pot.
3. Wash and cut leeks, also into bite sized shapes and sauté in olive oil until tender.
4. Place leeks in pot with potatoes and cover with water. Add salt to taste.
5. Boil gently for 45 minutes or until potatoes are soft. Do not over boil as the potatoes will dissolve in the hot water.
6. Add milk or cream to stock pot and garnish with parsley and pepper.
7. Serve heated with toast and butter, adding pepper to the serving bowl as desired. Can be reheated and stored in frig for several days.

Potato and Polish Sausage Soup

Ingredients

1 medium onion, chopped
5 tblsp olive oil

½ cup flour

6 medium potatoes

1 foot Polish sausage, chopped into bite sizes

3 ½ cups water

3 cups whole milk (or any other milk)

Salt and Pepper

Instructions

1. In a saucepan, sauté the onion in olive oil until caramelized. Remove onion from pan, placing into stock pot.

2. In pan where the onion was sautéed, add the flour and constantly stir flour while browning over low to medium heat. When flour is browned, set aside for cooling.

3. In stock pot, add 3 cups water to the onions, cubed Polish sausage and salt.

4. Cook on medium heat until potatoes are soft. When cooked, place remaining ½ cup of water in a small bowl with the browned flour and mix until smooth.

5. Add flour/water mixture to the hot stock pot and reduce to a simmer for 2 minutes.

6. Add milk and simmer for additional 5 minutes.

7. Add black pepper to taste and serve heated. Best served with toast.

Lamb Stew

Ingredients

1 lb of raw lamb, diced (can be any cut of lamb with the fat mostly removed)

6 medium potatoes (washed and peeled). If the potatoes are new, do not peel

2 carrots, chopped

1 large onion, chopped

2 pieces of celery stalks, chopped
1 clove garlic, crushed
Salt and Pepper
4 tbsp corn starch
½ cup cold water
4-6 cups water
½ cup chopped parsley

Instructions

1. Place lamb in roaster with 1 cup of water and place in oven at 300 degrees Fahrenheit for 2 hours.

2. When cooked, place all the lamb meat, including the juice along with potatoes, carrots, onions, celery, garlic and salt into a large stock pot and cover with the remaining 4-6 cups of water.

3. Boil gently for 40 minutes or until the potatoes and carrots are soft.

4. In a small bowl, combine ½ cup cold water, corn starch and some salt and pepper, mixing well to dissolve the corn starch. Pour mixture into hot pot of soup to thicken as desired. This step can be repeated to make the stew as thick a desired.

5. Garnish with parsley. Serve heated with fresh bread and butter or toast.

Variation:

a. Lamb can be replaced with any meat such as beef, chicken, pork.

b. Adding herbs such as peppermint, basil, thyme, savory, or sage will enhance the flavour of this stew.

11

FOLLOWING DREAMS

"You will never find time for anything. You must make it."
-- Charles Buxton

I'd thought about helping Grandma with canning the rhubarb and honey syrup jam that went so well with ice cream, but instead I got distracted by a phone call.

"Is this the granddaughter of Rosa Belle....?" sounded the voice on the other end of the line.

I hadn't even heard the rest of the sentence. "Yes," I replied.

"I'm very sorry," she said, "I have some bad news."

My heart pounded, my head felt light and I don't remember anymore words that were exchanged on that phone call. All I remember was hanging up the phone and screaming, "Oh God, give me more time!" I felt guilty that I hadn't spent even more time with my grandmother, and now, it might be too late. Why was I so absorbed with my own self, I wondered. But then I remembered some words, "Time is an illusion, Emma. Everyone has the same amount of time in a day and it's what you do with your time that defines your life." I wasn't sure who had first said that to me, but I did remember it well because it was relating to me how I spend my days and what I do with each day. Was I doing what I was born to do, or was I wasting my time with things that didn't matter to me in the end? How should I know what to spend my time on, I wondered?

And for the next twenty four hours while I sat by my grandmother's hospital bed, holding her hand, watching her face for movement with tubes coming from her nose and mouth and listening to the life support machine humming away, I thought about what she had told me about following my dreams while I have the time. When in doubt about what you want to do each day, follow your dreams. Dreams are the things life is made from and are the memorable parts of living an exciting and satisfying life. Without dreams, experiences can be harsh and seem meaningless, but dreams keep the days exciting, energizing and full of meaning. They can help to shape your attitude and therefore your personal contribution to each day. It was while sitting in that hospital room alongside the woman I loved most in the world that I consciously chose to make those words something to live by my whole life.

"God has opportunities for greatness for you everywhere, Emma," Grandma said repeatedly. No matter where you are, what you are doing or who you're with, God can use you to do His work if you let Him. He will guide you through all the obstacles in life giving your life meaning and purpose. Even the darkest hour can have God's hand in it if you let Him be there.

This lesson I had to keep reminding myself over and over. Sometimes my life seemed too mundane for what I liked and at other times, it seemed too overwhelming. It was a question of balance and matching my energy to my ambitions and my ambitions to my dreams.

Grandma had ambitions of her own but never really talked much about them. Mostly, she tended her gardens, gathered the harvest, preserved the food and worked at the hospital or nursing home. Her whole life seemed to be about home and work from what I could tell. She raised her family, had been married and I suppose, once upon a time, had a girl like ambition to be a mother and a grandmother, and the fantastic part to me is that Grandma really liked her life.

She would often say, "Having children is a blessing, but having grandchildren is an even bigger blessing. Grandchildren are God's reminder to older people to remember the priorities in life and to never become too serious. We must always be childlike and in God's eyes; it's his children whom He loves so much. The good news is," she continued, "we are all his children and so he loves us all equally and we must remember to ask Him for His guidance and to trust Him as our Father. You my dear; you are my grandchild and you are more precious to me than gold and you remind me to be childlike, starting each day with bright eyes and being thankful for all the gifts I receive, no matter the form they take."

Grandma was a positive thinker; there was never any doubt about that. When the bunny rabbits were born on her front step, Grandma said they too were blessings. She picked them up and brought them in as her own, fed the mother leafy greens ensuring mommy had enough nutrition herself to feed her babies and then when they were weaned, Grandma allowed the rabbit and her bunnies to decide on their own if they wanted to stay. Some did and some didn't. The ones who did were well fed and cared for and became part of Grandma's family, the others wandered off to find adventure of their own. She was magical with animals and children and that was God's way for Grandma. As Grandma said, "They're blessings."

Grandma was always concerned for animals, but she was sincerely concerned for the people around her and especially for those who had arthritis. Arthritis is such a crippling disease; it literally ruins so many people's dreams for life by limiting their mobility. So when my great aunt phoned to tell us she had been diagnosed with severe arthritis and that she would soon be unable to walk on her own, my grandmother shut down the kitchen and summoned me to the table where she and I were to share a cup of herbal tea and lament on how we were going to help her sister through this unexpected turn in life, just as God would want us to do.

"Aunt Agatha had more dreams than anyone I know. She loved to canoe and hike and snow shoe in the winter too. Cross country skiing came naturally to her and with her living out in the country where she does, she has lots of room to do it. Now what's she to do?" Grandma said staring into her tea cup as though the leaves would tell her the answer she so needed to hear.

"I don't know Grandma. Do you suppose she can sell her house and move into the city where she will have easy access to everything?" I asked.

"Maybe. I just don't know what her dreams will be made of now that she won't be able to move around quite so easily. It will hurt her so much to give up her life as she knows it."

"Does she have to give up on life?" I probed. "Can she do other things like arts and crafts? Maybe she'll become a famous painter or wood sculptor."

"Yes, I suppose she could, if she has the talent for it," Grandma tried to be encouraging but her tone of voice belied her words. I could tell she was very disappointed for her sister.

"What causes arthritis, Grandma?"

"Well, I suppose it's from any number of things. I remember from my training as a nurse that it comes as osteoarthritis and rheumatoid arthritis and they're both different but both can cause extreme discomfort. Osteoarthritis is a degenerative joint disease where the cartilage is not healthy and is degenerating. Cartilage acts as the shock absorber in the joint and when the 'shocks' wear down, the bones rub together which causes pain. Not a good thing because swelling can occur and then mobility is reduced. Collagen decreases in the body when you get older and it's this collagen that is used to keep the cartilage healthy, so without it, the joints naturally start to inflame when the cartilage wears down. My own grandmother used to eat ginger root to reduce the pain from her osteoarthritis. She also ate lots of cabbage and fresh berries because she said those made her feel better. I suppose they did too because they're filled with nutrition. Rheumatoid arthritis is different in that it's caused by the autoimmune function of the body. It too can be very painful. In both cases, a diet rich in fresh fruits and vegetables and essential fatty acids has helped a great number of people."

"I like to add gelatin to my diet naturally in the form of desserts, and main courses and maybe this is in part what has helped me to be free from arthritis in spite of my age," Grandma continued. "I eat plenty of fresh fruit, veggies and my saturated fat intake from animal meat is low because I'm particular about removing it and eating the lean meat that I raise on my own land. Of course, you know I love to eat fresh salmon too."

"I love my recipe for chicken soup," she continued. "The bones in the chicken have collagen in them naturally that can be seen when the soup broth is chilled and turns to jelly. All bones have collagen in them, and so I like to add them to my broths for their nutrition content. Of course, gelatin can be purchased either in bulk or by the small packages in the grocery store. I like to buy bulk to avoid the waste of packaging and because it's much less expensive."

My grandmother loved her soup. She had a warming and comforting soup recipe for every occasion and ensured there was a fresh pot made each week for everyone to snack from. One of the most unusual ones I remember her making was a chickpea and lentil soup that had an East

Indian flare to it. It was spicy and sour and had the warming spices so well known in Indian cooking. I'm not sure where she got the recipe from but knowing Grandma, I suspect she made it up herself by combining a few other recipes of her favourite spices and soups. At least, that's how I account for the fact that the ingredients are a unique combination of various cultures culminating into one delicious pot of soup. The spice is tantalizing to my taste buds and yet refreshing to my whole body. I do watch the amount of cayenne and black pepper I put in because although they're necessary for the full flavour to come through, they can be overwhelming causing me to cough if I'm not prepared for it. A nice piece of warmed bread is delicious with this meal.

Fruit Juice Gelatin for dessert

Ingredients

1 tbsp of gelatin powder

¼ cup of cold water

¼ cup of boiling water

2 cups of fruit juice or cocktail – Can use blueberry, apple or other non citrus fruit (citrus fruit won't set)

Instructions

1. Stir gelatin in small mixing bowl with the cold water.

2. Add boiling water to mixing bowl stirring until gelatin dissolved.

3. Stir in 2 cups of fruit juice.

4. Chill overnight or until set.

Chicken Soup with Gelatin

Ingredients

Whole chicken pieces with bones

2 large onions

1 whole clove of garlic

1 cup previously cooked pot of pearl barley

3 large carrots, chopped

1 head of broccoli, chopped

3 large peeled potatoes

4 stocks of celery, chopped

1 head of finely chopped parsley

Salt and pepper

3 5 tbsp of gelatin

Instructions

1. Boil whole chicken pieces with bones attached in a large stock pot for several hours with onions and garlic, using enough fresh water to fill pot ¾ full.

2. Chill stock for future use or continue making soup as described in following steps.

3. Carefully remove chicken from pot and once cooled, remove meat from bones and skin, saving the meat to add back to soup at end. Compost bones and skin.

4. Skim excess fat from top of liquid using a large spoon.

5. Add to the stock previously cooked pot of pearl barley, carrots, broccoli, potatoes, celery, parsley, and salt and pepper to taste if desired adding small amounts at a time.

6. Cook for 45 minutes on medium heat and then add deboned chicken.

7. Stir in 3 5 tbsp of gelatin (will dissolve in hot water).

8. Serve. Left over soup can be canned, frozen or stored in refrigerator for up to 3 days.

Variations

a. Broad egg noodles can be added.

b. Long grain rice can be used instead of or in combination with barley.

c. Any vegetable can be added or eliminated. Suggestions include, spinach, basil, Brussels sprouts, green beans, peas, bok choy.

d. Chicken can be replaced with any meat and bones like pork, beef, or lamb.

Chicken in Mushroom Sauce

Ingredients

1 can evaporate milk or 1½ cups fresh milk, any kind

2 tbsp flour or corn starch (if using fresh milk)

1 lb or 2 packages washed and sliced Mushrooms

4-5 pieces of skinless Chicken with bones attached (Boneless Breast fillets can also be used)

1 small onion

2 small pieces of fresh garlic

2 tbsp Gelatin powder

Salt and pepper to taste

2 Cups fully cooked rice

Fresh green vegetables of your choice

Instructions

1. In a blender, combine milk with ½ the mushrooms and if using fresh milk, add the flour or cornstarch. Add onion, fresh garlic and gelatin to blender and salt and pepper as desired.

2. Mix on medium speed until mushrooms are finely chopped.

3. Place washed chicken in an oven ready casserole dish or pan, pouring blender mixture over all pieces until fully covered.

4. Bake at 350 degrees Fahrenheit for 45 minutes or until top of milk mixture is a rich golden brown and chicken is fully cooked.

5. Serve over rice and add fresh vegetable such as broccoli or salad. Garnish with fresh parsley for colour and added nutrients such as

chlorophyll, vitamin C, flavonoids and carotenes.

TIP:

Keep left over chicken mushroom broth and serve as mushroom soup with fresh homemade bread. Broth can be refreshed by adding water and additional mushrooms in equal portions boiled together and seasoned to taste. Mix thoroughly and serve warm.

Chickpea and Lentil Soup

Ingredients

1 cup chickpeas

5 cups water

½ cup dried lentils or yellow split peas

4-6 large cloves garlic

1 tsp salt

3 bay leaves

1 small chopped onion

1 medium chopped carrot

2 stalks of chopped celery

¼ tsp cardamom

¼ tsp ground cayenne pepper

¼ tsp ground black pepper

Handful of chopped coriander leaves (can substitute 1 tsp of ground coriander)

1 tsp ground caraway seeds

1 tsp turmeric

1 tsp ground oregano

1 lemon- squeezed (using a citrus juicer)

4 tbsp extra virgin olive oil

2 tbsp gelatin

Chopped chives

Fresh Parsley

Fresh Peppermint leaves

Instructions

1. In a covered pot to avoid water from evaporating, BOIL chickpeas, lentils, garlic, salt, bay leaves, onion, carrot and celery in water on low heat until chickpeas are soft and lentils have dissolved (about 1 hour). TIP: Soak uncooked chickpeas in water overnight before boiling to reduce cooking time.

2. ADD cardamom, cayenne pepper, black pepper, coriander leaves, caraway seeds, turmeric, oregano, lemon juice, olive oil and gelatin.

3. SIMMER for 15 minutes.

4. SERVE hot and garnish each bowl with chives, parsley and peppermint leaf.

Grilled Salmon and Salad

Ingredients

Fresh Atlantic salmon, deboned and skin removed

Pinches of salt, garlic powder, onion powder, dried oregano, dried basil, dried thyme for seasoning salmon

Romaine Lettuce

Broccoli heads

Cucumber pieces

Tomato pieces

Fresh Dill

Fresh Basil

Fresh Cilantro

1 part Almond Oil/Olive Oil

1/2 part Raspberry Balsamic Vinegar

2 cloves Crushed Garlic

Instructions

1. Season the salmon.

2. Grill on hot griller for 8 minutes or until thoroughly cooked.

3. While salmon is grilling, combine washed lettuce, broccoli, cucumber, tomato, dill, basil and cilantro together making a salad.

4. Mix oil, vinegar and garlic together in a bottle. Shake well and add to salad.

5. Serve salmon hot and salad cold on one plate, garnishing with dehydrated herbs.

TIPS:

a. Salmon skin is easier to remove once cooked.

b. Season the grilled salmon on the flesh side for full flavour.

c. Using a salad spinner for washing lettuce and fresh herbs is convenient.

12

END OF SUMMER DELIGHTS

"As Rosemary is to the Spirit, so Lavender is to the Soul."
-- Anonymous

By end of summer, visiting Grandma's house was a delightful thing to do. She had the kind of porch that made you feel like you were rich and comfortable because it was large and roomy and had visible vantage points for viewing the surrounding area through the trees. Grandma hung potted flowers that swung from the ceiling when the wind flowed through. The porch had white wood spindles, and white Muskoka chairs like the ones people have on their cottage properties near their docks overlooking their beautifully peaceful lake. Large cushioned swing sets were surrounded by potted plants and were perfect for sitting on during warm summer nights. But on Grandma's porch, there was no end to the supplies of herbs and veggies she left there to dry out in the sun. Grandma would start cutting down her gardens in late August knowing that if the fall was warm, more would grow and she would get to harvest a second crop, called a bumper crop.

Visiting her most days, I climbed the steps to Grandma's wooden porch and picked through her harvested garden crops as though I were at a market. She would have dill weed drying across the arms of the chairs, tomatoes drying out on card board boxes soaking up the sun and dehydrating on their own and basil too. Some basil plants were in large bunches with roots soaking in pails of water keeping them fresh for homemade pesto. The peppers too, would dehydrate in the sun and the seeds from each item were harvested, dried and packaged into envelops for planting in the ground the following spring.

Grandma especially loved her herb and spice garden. She grew several kinds of oregano, parsley, thyme, basil, red hot chilli peppers, chives, garlic, leeks and green onions. Grandma said all her recipes were the special combinations of her favourite herbs and vegetables. Having potatoes, pasta and rice were the essentials, she told me, with the flair, the colour and the flavour coming from the herbs and spices.

"Combining all your favourites into one dish won't harm your meal, it will enhance it. Your taste buds will thank you for it and so will your entire body when it digests all the goodness and nutrients from your herbs," Grandma explained to me.

"Herbs have so many nutrients in them they can help with disease prevention such as arthritis, heart disease, blood pressure, circulation issues and cancers, and the best part is, when you grow them yourself, they don't have chemicals that can cause the body harm. Water them with fresh, clean water, and if the bugs and animals eat your plants in the summer, then consider yourself blessed that they've chosen your garden from which to eat. That means it's good food.' She continued on with, 'Keep your faith and you will know that you're doing God's will to help His critters be alive and well fed. You will get more than you need to feed yourself from your garden so there's never a reason to be greedy with it. Share it abundantly."

Grandma was the epitome of someone who shared and all her neighbours knew it, which is why I believe that when Grandma fell on some hard times, she had friends who cared for her and provided her with help. This certainly was true for her when Grandma had been hurt by a fall from her extension ladder while painting the window frames on her house. She not only fell on hard times, she fell on hard ground. Faithfully, her neighbours continued to grow Grandma's gardens and feed her animals while she herself was laid up with leg and back injuries.

Going through surgeries trying to repair the damage that had been done to her strong bones by the fall, Grandma used the knowledge she had of the body to help with her own healing. She exercised her muscles daily by stretching and using her body weight to rebuild her strength. All day long, Grandma exercised, rested and healed until a few months later, she was able to walk out of the hospital on her own two feet. It still took Grandma well over a year to finish healing and getting her full strength back, but she did it. "Today, Emma, you have Pilates and yoga so available to you, but in my day, those things weren't really heard of. Pilates though, I had heard of that during the war when I was a nurse and I saw with my very own eyes, those war amputees living because of doing the exercises with the bed springs. That doctor was a smart one, inventing a way of strengthening your own body while lying in bed, being barely able to move. Before he came along, so many people just laid there and then died because there wasn't enough circulation to their joints and throughout their bodies and therefore no blood flowing like it has to in order to heal. Did you know,' Grandma continued, 'that it's the nutrients and oxygen in the blood that get carried around the body to all the body parts that heals the body? Well it does. And when this doctor came and showed everyone how to use strengthening exercises for the muscles, allowing the circulation to flow, it was then that people started to heal. People were able to strengthen their stomach muscles enough so they could sit up from a lying position using their own strength after just a few days of working with this amazing doctor. The whole hospital cheered each time one of those men left that place using their own strength instead of being carried out in one of those horrible bags, leaving to be buried."

And so when Grandma returned to her home after being released from the hospital, she thanked all her neighbours who had cared for her gardens, animals and property while she was away. And she continued to thank them each time she brought to them a homemade casserole or rice pilaf made from her garden herbs. Grandma loved sharing her nutritious food with those she loved and she loved her neighbours.

Making large batches of rice pilaf, Grandma left it in her refrigerator for quick suppers and light lunches on demand. Before she owned a microwave, Grandma reheated the rice mixture in a sauce pan and sometimes added an egg to it for protein and variety.

Soya sauce and sesame oil are my favourite garnishes as well as hot crushed chillies. I've always enjoyed eating this rice dish oriental style, with chop sticks and holding the bowl up to my chin and quite often dropping most of my food back into the bowl.

"A great way of preserving garden food is to dehydrate it, Emma," Grandma taught me. "Wash it first though, while it's fresh and pliable. Spin it out in a salad spinner and then set it aside on a tea towel for drying. It will take about a week, but then it can be transferred to a paper bag and stored for a couple of years in a dry place. Or, it can be tied with butcher cord at its ends to form bunches for storage. In this way, it can be rolled between the palms of your hands to release the herbs into the cooking pot."

I now own a dehydrator for quickly drying my food, but my grandma did it the old fashioned way using no electricity and it worked perfectly fine. My dehydrator is green in colour, but not the green of Grandma's ways.

Garden Rice

This version of Rice Pilaf is a dish that is your own original creation and should be made with the ingredients you love to eat.

Ingredients

2 cups of long grain rice, well rinsed

4 cups of water

Pinch of salt

1/8 cup Sesame or Olive Oil

Soya Sauce, of your liking

Homemade liquid Hot Sauce (optional)

Any selection of the following fresh herbs and vegetables according to your liking:

Basil leaves

Thyme leaves

Any variety of lettuce such as romaine, butter, or leaf

Green onions

Yellow or white onion

Chives

Parsley

Banana, green, red bell, or hot chili peppers

Spinach/chard/kale

Instructions

1. Boil water and then add rice.

2. Reduce heat to a simmer for 20-30 minutes, allowing for the water to be absorbed and the texture to be the way you like it. For softer rice, remove from heat earlier, for firmer rice, allow water to evaporate more by leaving on the simmering heat longer.

3. While rice is cooking, prepare your favourite vegetables and herbs from the garden by washing and chopping as desired. For peppers, onions, celery and other hard vegetables, chop into chunks and set aside. For

leafy and soft herbs and vegetables such as lettuce chard, spinach, etc, leave whole or break into large sections.

4. When all the herbs and vegetables are washed and prepared by dicing, place these uncooked items into a large serving bowl.

5. Add the hot rice on top and allow it to sit for a brief time, 1 minute, cover if desired. Adding the hot rice on top of the uncooked garden food will have a blanching effect on them and will heat them enough for eating. Doing it this way will help to ensure all the plant enzymes remain intact.

6. Mix together the ingredients in the serving bowl with large serving spoons for a uniform mixture.

7. Garnish with soy sauce and homemade hot sauce if desired.

8. Pour on sesame oil or olive oil for additional flavour and added health benefits.

Variation:

Add sautéed meat to the rice dish for a complete meal. Chicken, pork and beef slices/chunks are perfect additions. Being creative in how the meat is prepared will enhance this dish to gourmet standards.

Tomato Chips

Tomato chips are an excellent snack in place of potato chips or can be used in soups, salads and pastas simply by rehydrating the chips in some warm water.

Ingredients

Tomatoes

Instructions

1. Wash and slice ripened tomatoes, removing any blotchy areas.

2. Place in dehydrator on individual racks being careful not to overlap tomatoes.

3. Dehydrate until desired consistency (about 6 hours on medium heat).

4. Chips can be stored in plastic bags or containers in refrigerator for very long periods of time, depending on dryness.

TIPS:

a. For use in pasta dishes, add tomato chips to pot of boiling pasta and they will rehydrate.

b. Tomatoes are also great in soups: In a blender, combine 4-6 freshly washed and quartered tomatoes with 1 cup of water. Pour into pot. Add fresh or dried basil, oregano or thyme. Heat to serve.

Variations

Add 1 freshly cut carrot and/or red pepper without the seeds to blender with tomatoes and water and heat to serve as above. Any dried or fresh herb can be added to your liking. TIP: This mixture made in large quantities is easily canned and will make a refreshing and hydrating lunch for the entire year. It can be made in the fall season when tomatoes are abundant.

13

GRANDMA HAD A UNIQUE PERSPECTIVE ON LEADERSHIP

"Where there is no vision, the people perish."
-- Proverbs 29:18

Coming home from work one afternoon expecting to be washing and slicing tomatoes, preparing them for the food dehydrator and making the most delicious tomato chips, I found Grandma standing in her kitchen bent over the counter. She had already carried the entire half bushel of tomatoes in from the garage, had them all washed and was almost finished slicing and layering the pieces neatly in a roasting pan, when I walked in.

"You were later than usual coming home, so I thought I'd get a head start on the tomatoes," she explained. "What kind of day did you have?"

"A tough one," I said. "More of the same nonsense going on with using the processes that I was hired to fix, but when I do fix them, the people executing on them don't get it."

"What don't they get?"

So I began to tell her, "People don't get that progression requires things to change. And it requires the people to change their way of thinking and their way of doing things, like their habits. The most common complaint I hear from people is, 'she doesn't listen'. Yet whenever I review the discussions, emails and whisperings of what I'm not listening to, I see clearly that I have listened. I've heard what they said, I've gone away to think about it and then I've considered their input when developing the newly created processes and plans used to improve things for the people working there. I then revisit other issues that are out there, for clarity checks, as I call them, and yes, there's stuff that I disregard in my plans because they're either archaic thinking, or they don't fit into the new plans. They're ideas that got the group into the weeds in the first place and don't work to get them untangled. In fact, down the road, doing what they want will lead to even more complications and further entanglement in the weeds, whereas my job is to untangle those weeds. What they're missing is; I'm not doing what they say, and they're translating that to I'm not listening. Of course, I'm listening, but I'm not going to do what they say if it's not the right thing to do. I was hired for my particular skill set to untangle things for that department and doing things their way won't get them untangled. They should be 'listening' to me, using their definition of the word 'listen'."

Sighing, my grandmother put down her paring knife and turned to look at me.

"What?" I asked with a light laughter in my voice.

"Being a manager can be a thankless job, Emerald. No matter whether you're good at managing processes and leading people through them or whether you're bad at it, all the blame for things that go wrong is yours because you're accountable. Odd thing is; if you're really good at being a manger, the credit doesn't typically come your way, it goes to your staff. A really good manager will empower their staff so they can do a great job. The credit will then go to the staff because they're the ones doing the work which is what people are measuring. But what people really remember is how they felt about the changes you were leading them through. Your job is to help them through it. And once you've successfully led your staff through the changes, observers will start saying things about your staff like, 'isn't so and so just great. They have so much passion and enthusiasm; they're doing such a great job.'

The good manager will give the credit to the staff knowing that in an environment that has a bad manager, that same person probably wouldn't be performing to those high standards. It was you who provided those opportunities and you must take comfort in that fact," Grandma offered.

"A practice that great managers can use," she carried on, "is to manage the processes and then lead the people through them. In that way, people will experience the change and learn what they are to do and will become comfortable taking the path you create for them. It's kind of like building a new and smoothly paved road that takes off from the old bumpy stone road. If people know there's a new road and they feel safe, then they'll take it. Alternatively, if they don't know the new road exists or they don't know that it's safe, no matter how you try to steer them on to it, they'll resist. They'll choose the old road instead because it's familiar. This is natural behaviour."

"I suggest you try and tap into what's natural to people and then you won't have to work so hard at change. People will begin to follow your processes if they come to them naturally. Remember that change can be viewed as unsafe because it can be the great unknown that feels uncomfortable or worse, leads to experiences and feelings they've never had before or fear having. You as the manager can build on familiar and safe experiences. In this way, people will follow your lead using your new processes."

Picking her knife back up to continue cutting the tomatoes, Grandma went on with, "If you want people to follow your lead, they have to feel safe with you. They have to believe you will help them and they have to believe you will make their life easier. People want to enjoy themselves and relax in their environment. They want to perform well and they want to be empowered to make the decisions that are theirs to make. But to do so, they must trust their leaders."

"If you want to feel what I'm saying, let's use visualization. Think of a time when a politician was announcing their intention to run for a party. Firstly, think of a leader who you didn't like, and ask yourself why you didn't like them. Use visualization to imagine where you were and what you were doing on a day when you heard from that leader, and really feel how you felt. Close your eyes if you wish to do so helping you to really feel and see the moment."

Waiting a few moments before speaking to me again, Grandma allowed me time to visualize this event. I visualized standing in the shopping mall at the book stand, seeing the face of a politician on the cover. He had already been in power for one term and was about to announce his nomination to run for a second. The economy had been a mess during his time in power and many people lost their jobs and homes because of it. A cold feeling came over me then, and I shivered. The shiver went right up my spine, into my shoulders and through my arms. Quickly, I opened my eyes and I recentered myself in Grandma's kitchen.

"How are feeling right now?"

"Cold and scared," I replied.

"Now consider the opposite, and think of a leader who you do like and ask yourself why you like them? Do the same and close your eyes to visualize."

This time I visualized another man who was about to announce his candidacy in the next election. He was a leader new to the political scene, but had a family history steeped in politics. I knew very little about him, but I did have a visual of his face and I did know what his family history was and what the family did when they were in politics and head of the country. It was during that time, the economy went strong, social reform occurred and people were generally happy. Thinking about this, I felt my shoulders start to relax, my body posture softened and a warm feeling over came me. I then realized I had been hunched over and began to straighten my spine, standing up taller. Wow, I was instantly breathing easier and feeling lighter. My eyes popped open and I was almost dizzy, I felt so good.

"So how are you feeling now?" she asked.

"I feel warm and happy and, something else."

"Would you want to be around that leader?" she probed inquiringly.

"Yes, I would definitely want to be around them. But I also don't feel like I would have to be around them. I feel like I could completely forget they were there and that no matter what decisions they were making, I could trust them to make the right ones. I feel, well, I feel safe." Slowly the word safe came out of my mouth and my grandmother's point hit home.

I wondered if the people who work with me feel safe about the decisions I make for them. Am I being a good enough leader where they can take their eyes off me and trust that the decisions I make for them are leading them to a better place, or am I scaring them with my new processes leaving them feeling unsafe and uncomfortable? I will have to evaluate my leadership style while leading everyone through the new processes, removing the fears that might be rooted deep within them. Fears I don't even know exist, and fears that will be different for everyone.

Laughingly, I decided Grandma is smart, and a good leader.

And with that, she and I carried on with slicing the tomatoes for the dehydrator making my favoured tomato chips.

Having sincere vision and actually seeing where I wanted my group to be in two, five and seven years from now was something I valued. At work, I laid out plans and strategies of how I would get them there and was determined to ensure they all participated in the journey. I learned this skill from my mom who knew how to share her vision with the people around her, making it their own vision and so they truly did become engaged in making things happen eventually, and with positive outcomes. They were prepared to give all their energy to a defined purpose. This talent of a shared vision was true for recreational activities too, such as the baseball team I was on. Building teams in the house league was done by stacking good players on a team, making that team strong and then leaving other teams to defeat. It was a practice that had been going on for some time, but no one could stop this from happening. The teams were supposed to be populated by the kids living in the area of their home district, but deals were often made and players were traded to stronger teams. Adult egos were in the way of the kids having fun, and the coaches made the games difficult. One particular season, my own mother decided to coach a team having sat on the benches as a parent for a few years while she watched me play ball. It was one of the few fun activities in my life she shared in and the most memorable. She decided she could use her skills she practiced at her office for the betterment of my team and so volunteered to be the coach, but not just of any team. She wanted the underdog team, the team that had the most losses the year before. Laughing at her, the house league gave her the team with the most losses from the year before, the team I was on, and mom set her shared vision on us so her vision became our vision. She taught us basic catching, throwing, hitting, ground ball stopping techniques as well as team playing strategies like who would back up whom and how each person would cover another's position. She taught us basic strategy plays and then had us practice them until we knew them in our sleep. She said this training would make our skills strong and the plays would become natural to us during a real game when our emotions were high and the games were intense. She said that if we knew what we were doing ahead of time, we would instinctively make plays that stopped the other team from making runs. It was their runs that would make us lose a game, she told us. After learning how to make outs while playing in the field, she taught us how to earn our own runs so we would score and win the game. Mom had the strategy and the plan to get us there and she wanted to make winning our vision so we would execute on the plan with her coaching us on the sidelines.

"It's you who will make the plays," Mom coached, "I will stand here overseeing the big picture and encouraging you to run or stop and reminding you what drill you will be using in real play. But it's you who will win the game, together as a team. Losses will be there too, but the losses only help us to learn what our weaknesses are so we can turn them into strengths for the important games. Losses will show which drills we'll have to practice more of and they will serve to keep us on our toes so we don't become complacent while other teams come up from behind and steal away our championship. Instead, we will be the team who sneaks up on the stronger teams while they sit comfortably thinking they are dominant in the league. They will be focused on each other and we will quietly overtake them before they become aware of our challenge, and by then, it will be too late for them. The plan, then, will be for us to stop their runs into home, and scoring points, while making runs of our own, thereby winning the championship." Mom had a plan.

And it was with this shared vision, that we as a team, practiced, drilled and celebrated together each winning game and continually learned from each losing game. We weren't bad at playing ball, we just had skills and techniques to learn before we could become a championship team. Sometimes we had lots of fun together on the field and sometimes, we were cold and wet if the day had been overcast and rainy, and that wasn't so much fun. Mom, I mean the coach, took us for ice cream on occasion and we enjoyed eating our cones and bonded together as friends with a shared purpose of having fun first and winning the championship next, or least be as good of a team as we could be. The important thing was, we all shared the same common goal.

"I'm going to test each of your skills in the areas of hitting the baseball, catching it, and throwing it, as well as your speed at running," Mom told us on practice day. "And then, I'm going to assign you to a field position and batting order based on your skills so you compliment the entire team. It's important you understand that each person is a valued member of the team and each of you has a skill that the team will use. For the skill you are strongest at, you must stay strong in that skill area and the team will count on you to be the lead in that area when it's your turn to play."

Mom made each of us feel like at some time in every game, each one of us was the most important person on that team and for that moment, we were. It was our turn to 'pull' the team along using our strength and newly found skills. She ensured each one of us knew what we were good at and how we were to use that skill and most importantly, when we were to use it. She would say things like, now, it's your turn or, you can do this, or go, go, go. And sure enough, because each of us knew there were other team mates counting on us at that moment, we gave it our best. We cheered each other on when a run was counted or a fly ball was caught and loved it when a runner from the opposite team was tagged as out. We empathized with those on our team who missed the fly catch or failed to make it to base or struck out at the plate, but we didn't let them off the hook, no way, they were a big part of the team and we were there to help them get better and stronger at things they were good at. The house league had a rule that no player could sit out the entire game so every girl played at least half the

107

game meaning we all had to improve in areas that weren't natural to us. It helped me to understand the concept of team building and from that, I felt I was part of the bigger picture, of something more powerful than just I, part of the universe where there were things beyond my control, and where great things could be accomplished.

"How did you learn to coach baseball, Mom?" I asked her one day while driving home from a practice.

Mom shrugged her shoulders, and then said, "I didn't so much as learn how to coach baseball. I learned how to recognize and develop people's strengths, and I learned that from your grandmother. Your grandma could see God's gifts in people and she admired what they were good at, pointing it out to them. I watched as she told people what she really liked about them and I watched their body postures change when Grandma told them good things about what she saw. They became more confident and smiled and their eyes shone brighter and they participated more in what Grandma was doing. It was positive reinforcement for them and they liked being part of a team and having shared experiences with other people when they thought they could contribute. And so, for baseball, I learned the necessary rules of the league and of the game in general and applied those rules to people who genuinely wanted to learn and contribute to the game. After all, that's why they were there, to play ball and be part of a team. I focused in on their desires and then showed them what they're good at and I told them the team was counting on them, which made them feel important for a brief time. It caused elation in them when they succeeded. The important part is in knowing they didn't have to be great at everything because someone else would have the strengths they didn't and so this relieved the pressure from them. They could have down time, as I like to call it, where they only had to be decent at the other skills required for the game but not excel at them. And if that failed, I made them laugh. Laughter relieves people of their tension and helps to promote relaxation of the muscles freeing the mind of clutter, making it easier to be comfortable and to play ball. People forget the missed catches and the strike outs when they laugh and they concentrate on the present, which is called the present because it's a gift. Laughter too, is a gift and has a way of healing hurts. And as you know, we also go for ice cream."

That was a loaded answer and at that time, I'm not sure I understood everything she said, but I did understand the part about making people laugh and I certainly understood the part about going for ice cream. That was my favourite part.

All in all, Mom's coaching paid off and we became the championship team that year, taking the league by surprise and taking home the trophy. We had worked hard, had lots of fun, made new friends and became the best team in the league while doing it. Now that's good leadership.

Homemade Ice Cream

Ingredients

Vanilla

1 cup heavy cream
1 tbsp vanilla
1 egg
¼ cup sugar

Instructions

1. In a blender, combine the above ingredients together on medium speed.
2. Pour into individual freezer safe dishes, cover and let sit until frozen, about 4 hours.
3. Remove from freezer and let sit until slightly softened.

4. For creamier ice cream, freeze entire mixture into one larger bowl and once softened, mix with a hand mixer. This will make a soft ice cream.

Preferred Method:

For those of you who have an ice cream machine, use the above recipe and slowly freeze in the maker following the directions of the manufacturer.

Variations:

a. Use plain or fruit yogurt, of any kind, instead of heavy cream.

b. Add 2 tbsp cocoa powder for chocolate ice cream or use liquid chocolate syrup to desired taste.

c. Add any fruit such as strawberries, blueberries, cherries, melons, etc, but be sure to blend the fruit in the blender first with some cream to make it smooth and delicious before freezing.

d. Ice Cream bars can be made using molds and popsicle sticks. Simple pour the mixture into the mold, insert the stick and allow time to freeze.

14

GREEN IS MY FAVOURITE COLOUR

"Green is the prime color of the world, and that from which its loveliness arises."
-- Pedro Calderon de la Barca

"Don't take this exit, I just read the sign that said road is closed due to construction", my mother bellowed out to me while lifting her head to look out the window and interrupting the story I was telling her about my most recent shopping experience.

"What?" I asked, focusing on my driving.

"Don't take this exit to get downtown, the sign said the road is closed for construction."

"Oh. Then I'll take the next one." Pointing at the next sign with my finger, I indicated that I had seen the ramp was closed confirming she was right and that construction work was indeed going on. "Of course this means that now we have to take the road that's narrow and has lots of stop lights and cars."

"What other choice do we have without going so far out of our way?' she asked.

"True," I replied, surrendering to what I thought would be a long and annoying drive due to the amount of traffic. By continuing the story where I'd left off before she interrupted me with the road closure, I actually distracted myself and began to enjoy the trip into the city again. I loved going into the city where the restaurants served great food, the shopping is exciting and the buildings have beautiful architecture. Signs of green energy and green space appeared on bill boards and I was reminded of the movement to use our energy wisely being green about everything we can.

Grandma was green. She had a green thumb, green gardens, green grass, green coat, green eyes and a green painted kitchen. It was Grandma's favourite colour. She always told me, "green has such magnificent energy and it's the colour of growth! Green is life giving and harmonizing. It affects the heart chakra and is related to loving oneself unconditionally and it helps us to love others in a balanced way, relieving stresses in our life allowing us to live with vitality."

"So what about the phrase 'green with envy?" I challenged her one day, provoking the conversation.

"That's a negative effect of the colour green," Grandma replied, always quick witted and well informed. "Green can sometimes be thought of as promoting jealousy, indifference and miserliness. But we must never dwell on those negative aspects, but rather on the positive ones which will invoke fertility, hope, peace and new life. In that way, we invite good karma into our lives."

Grandma never tired of talking about the earth or the country of her ancestors. "The word gronja was used in Germany by my ancestors like we use the word green today and it was used to brighten up a room."

"Is that why you painted your kitchen green, Grandma, because you wanted to remember your family?"

"Maybe. I do miss them a lot and wish those horrible things hadn't happened to them. But, Emma, I have you and for that, I am blessed. I want you to grow strong and healthy and with that, I know you will be beautiful on the inside. I then want you to share your beauty with others in the way of kindness. You will have the green beauty that grows from within you and people will notice it, but not all will know what they are seeing. They will only know they are enamoured by you."

Snapping from my reverie, I remind myself that I'm on my way into the city taking my mother with me for her cancer examine and treatment schedule.

Last year she was diagnosed with breast cancer and the doctor said she had a very high chance of living but that she would have to work at it and stay strong enough for the treatments. He told her she would have to really want to live to find the strength and energy to beat this.

At first the treatments consisted of radiation therapy, but that burnt my mother's chest and the pain she experienced from it was described to me as being worse than any sun burn I could ever imagine. After a few months of radiation treatment, Mom thought she was in remission and could then carry on with her life as usual. The sad thing was, the diagnosis was incorrect and the cancer was still there only this time it was stronger and larger than before and too large an area for radiation treatment. Surgery had to be done and her breast had to be removed. And so it was to be. Mom underwent a breast removal surgery and today I was taking her back to the hospital for her examination. We were both nervous because we knew a negative prognosis would likely mean death for my mother and neither of us was ready for that. There was still so much living to be done and I wasn't ready to lose my mom. And so, we distracted ourselves the entire way into the city talking about all the commotion going on and the traffic and the buildings in site right until we reached the cancer clinic where we both stopped talking completely. Sitting in the parked car, I looked over at my mother and stared into her warm brown eyes seeing so much love and yet fear too. I will always remember her gaze that's permanently etched into my brain.

"I love you, Mom," was all I could muster.

"I love you, too," she replied. And with that, we hugged for several minutes even though our backs were being twisted by the car seat.

Slowly we got out of the car and made our way to the clinic where we waited for our turn to see the doctor.

"Did you see all those buildings out there?" Grandma exclaimed.

I was day dreaming again to help ease the tension of the wait and so I was remembering the day I had brought my grandmother into the city to see a play. Something she had never done before. Staring at my Grandma after her comment, I saw the amusement of a child in her as she took in the big city sites. She and I went into the city to see a play at the theatre on King St in Toronto and this was the first time my grandmother had ever been there. She was marvellous! She took in all the big city sites admiring art work, glass buildings, tall buildings, old buildings, crowds, subways, traffic and shopping. Grandma was fortunate that the hotel we stayed at was located in the city's shopping center so taking the elevator to the basement led us to beautiful shopping centers, restaurants and the subway. Stopping at the banking machine to get some cash, Grandma noticed the coffee shop with the gourmet coffee selections located just across the hall and knowing it's my favourite coffee suggested we stop there to get a treat. Grandma always knew just what I wanted and at the right time too. Oh, how I wish I could have some of that coffee now.

"Mrs Jones?" The nursing assistant called, snapping me back to reality.

"Mom, that's us," I nudged her lightly and helped her to stand. "Do you want me to come in with you?"

Nodding, she acknowledged she wanted the support and we were led into the doctor's office.

"Mrs Jones," the doctor started, "I want you to know that we usually don't see cases like this. We thought we had it all and then we discovered there was more and yet, now we're seeing there's no cancer, at all. You're in complete remission."

The breath released from both Mom and I at exactly the same time and the noise we made was deafening. Turning to her again, I stood and grabbed her into my arms hugging and squeezing her hard. Grandma had been right. Green gardens held magical healing powers and were filled with nutrition. And so, we would be together for a while longer, God willing. God had worked through the doctors, nurses and technicians, for whom we are grateful.

The drive home that afternoon was light, blissful and full of joy. We marvelled at all the trees and brush growth along the highway as we traveled back to our home town to tell the good news to Grandma. And when we saw Grandma, she too hugged her daughter and led us into her kitchen for a fresh garden salad and a pot of tea.

<u>Green Salad:</u>

Ingredients

Fresh cut lettuce of any variety
Fresh spinach
Fresh basil, chives, thyme, dill and oregano
Broccoli sprouts, leaves and flower
Fresh tomatoes
Fresh cucumber
1 part each of Almond oil and olive oil for a total of 2 parts
1 parts apple cider vinegar

Instructions

1. Cut and wash ingredients and place in salad spinner to dry.

2. Top with: Tomatoes, Cucumber.

3. Mix almond oil, olive oil, and apple cider vinegar. Pour onto salad.

<u>Variations:</u>

a. For a cream salad dressing, add a tablespoon of mayonnaise to the above recipe and then pour onto salad.

b. Add grilled chicken, beef or salmon. Serve meat hot or cold with salad.

c. Add peppers, olives and feta cheese for additional flavour and nutrients.

15

GARDENING AND THE BEAST

"No disease that can be treated by diet should be treated with any other means."
-- Maimonides

I honestly thought my mother would beat the beast of disease, and in the end, she did. My mother lived. For my grandmother, the whole ordeal was a very difficult period. "No mother should ever live to bury her child," she muttered. And to have not had to do that, she was grateful.

When the vegetables in the garden flourished each summer, Grandma picked the crops clean and kept them for winter storage. The root veggies went into the cold cellar, the cucumbers were pickled, the peas, zucchini, squash, beans and peppers were dehydrated and then stored for use in soups, salads, casseroles or ground up and used as spices on top of meats and in slow cooker recipes.

Grandma was resourceful with all her food and chose never to waste it. Once a crop was finished, she pulled the plants out of the ground placing them in her compost pile and then planted new seeds. She only did this up to the end of July knowing the summer growing season could be long enough to support double crops. Bumper crops, Grandma called them.

Today, Grandma is replanting radishes, and zucchini's. Her radishes this year were the largest and reddest I'd ever seen.

"It's in the way you treat your plants, Emma that will determine how much they give to you and how healthy they will be." Grandma thought her plants were precious and told them so. She loved talking to them claiming they could hear her. "They have energy and give energy and feel energy, so if you love them and are good to them, they in turn, will be good back to you."

"Grandma?" I asked, "Do you ever love a plant, treating it well, but then doesn't it turn out healthy?"

"Yes, sometimes. Occasionally a mold, mildew, or bug will get to the plant and if I can catch it in plenty of time, then I can help the plant out. But if I don't catch it and whatever the nuisance is takes it over, then I may have to cut some of the leaves off, or worse, pull the plant out by the roots to let the healthy plants grow.

Just last week, I pulled seven cucumber plants out of the garden because the leaves had turned yellow. I think they'd been planted too close together and when the plants got large trying to grow, they competed with one another for space and the weaker plants got pushed out, receiving little amounts of water and nourishment and so they didn't grow very well. The leaves got weak and the plants starting dying. The cucumbers that did grow were small and funny shaped. My mother once told me that I would be able to tell how healthy the root was in a plant by looking at the vegetables growing from it. If the vegetables were distorted in shape, then likely the roots were being damaged. This could also be from bugs, and insects in the ground, and not always from overcrowding. The weaker plants have to be pulled allowing room for the stronger ones."

Helping Grandma collect all the vegetation and weeds pulled from the garden, I neatly piled them on the compost pile, thinking that next summer, I would be helping her by shovelling all this back into the garden as it would be soil by then. What a miracle, really, to think that everything goes back to the soil from where it came. The thought of death over came me at that moment thinking about the words I'd heard at a funeral, 'ashes to ashes, dust to dust' and I related those words to these plants. From soil to plant and then back to soil. Once again, I felt chills run up my spine as my body shivered. "God, please save my soul," I whispered, "and protect me from all anxiety. And forgive me all my sins. Thank you, God." Bending down to pick up the garden gloves, I felt warm again and breathed in the fresh summer air.

Grandma fed my mother well, but my mother didn't turn out healthy. Similarly to the plants that had to be pulled from the garden because they had been diseased, my mother too was almost pulled from the earth due to disease. She almost rested with God much too early in life and I often wondered why He had spared her life. I wondered if my mother still had things on earth to do, things that were God's work. I take comfort in thinking that God still had something more for her because my faith is so strong and I do love her. One day, He will take her and He'll take me too and then I'll will be with both my parents again and all my family who have gone before me. But the truth is, I really like being alive and so I want to live a very long time.

Before she became sick, I thought my mother would be around forever. I hadn't ever pictured life without her and so I was certain she would beat the beast and live, but that was naïve thinking, I know that now. It could have taken her life then, and I might have missed so much of our lives together. My mother did go on to live longer and had the chance of becoming a grandmother to my children, and she was quite good at it too. What she may have lacked in maternal care, she more than made up for in grandmother care. The children loved being around her and found joy in the times they shared. My mother showed a simple side to the children, playing with them, finding laughter in their voices and smiles on their dirty, chubby faces. God granted us so many blessings.

16

GREEN IS MY FOOD IN ABUNDANCE

"I feel more confident than ever that the power to save the planet rests with the individual consumer." -- Denis Hayes

It was after my mother's experience with cancer that I began really noticing the power of food and the abundance of it where I lived, knowing this was not so true for other areas in the world.

Walking from the newly built local grocery store, I noticed a sign as I pushed the shopping cart along the walkway to the roadway where I was parked. The sign read, 'shopping cart wheels will lock up if cart removed beyond this point.'

Huh? What could that mean I wondered as I continued walking and pushing my cart. I've never seen that before and then just at that moment, my cart wheels jammed and wouldn't travel any further. Letting out a laugh, I said out loud, "Oh, that's what that means," following up with a chuckle but not really thinking it was too funny. I mean, I now have a cart full of heavy groceries and the car is still around the corner and out of sight. Just how would I get my groceries to the car, I asked myself?

Guardian angels have a way of delivering help just when needed, and today was no different. Lingering by the sign checking to see what I was struggling with was a young man who had walked by me only moments before. Help, I thought, I really need this man's help. And so with humbleness, I asked him if he would help me to carry my groceries to my car and thanks to this man's great heart, he said yes. I was so happy he agreed to help me and that he didn't just walk by saying he was too busy. And mostly, I was happy I could trust this man to carry my groceries with me and not run off with them. It felt good to be safe in what was potentially a vulnerable situation and I will always remember this young man as a promise that there are so many good people out there. Thank you, whoever you are.

Later that evening as I lied in bed thinking about the new grocery store and all its products and clean bright aisles, it occurred to me just how much food was in that one store and when I thought about how many stores there were just like that one in my area, I thought about how much food must go to waste. Our town couldn't possibly buy and then eat that much food before its expiry dates, including those products with longer dates. I thought about all the fruits and vegetables and bread that must rot and have to be discarded. And I thought the same thing about all the dairy products like milk, yogurts, creams and eggs that I thought wouldn't have a use once their shelf life had expired. And what about all the meat, would these be the products that animal food is made from?

I'm sure someone knows the answer, but it's not me. I think about my gardens and the amount of food I now have in my house that makes me not be dependent so much on these grocery stores, yet I still go to them because I have some fixation on food. What is it about food that I love so much? Why do I have every cupboard filled with items to make things with thinking I'm about to starve. My house is generally lean when I compare it other people's houses that I know of, and yet it still has a pantry filled with pastas, rice, sauces, homemade preserves, canned meats and fruits all of which would sustain me for months of eating, and still, I travel to the grocery store two to three times a week. I will have to think about why I do that.

My mother did die eventually but not from the breast cancer as we all thought would take her life. Instead, she had heart disease; atherosclerosis is what they called it. She suffered with pain for a while and then one day, died. I found her lying on her couch with the TV on as though she was still watching it, her eyes wide open and her body covered with a warm blanket. It seemed to me like it was a peaceful death, but then one never knows what someone goes through on their way to meet their maker. Seeing her lying there, I wished I had spent more time with her and now that won't happen. Now I will make the funeral arrangements and let her rest in peace with my father. At least I have children to keep me strong.

Several months after the funeral and standing in the bathroom looking into the mirror, I brushed through my long brown hair looking for smoothness and shine while checking for split ends. "None, good," I said out loud but to no one in particular. Going through these simple motions and feeling down about my mother's death, I began remembering the times I spent in my grandmother's bathroom while growing up and thought about a day similar to this one when I had also been brushing out my hair, feeling down about life. This at least, took my mind off my mother.

"You look beautiful, Emerald," Grandma had smiled at me through the mirror as she passed by.

"You always say that to me, Granny."

"That's my job, to make you see you're great. And besides, it's true. You are beautiful on the inside and this beauty shines through to the outside. It's in your hair, your skin and your eyes. They all glow."

Looking closely into my eyes I could see the shine she spoke of. But the body to me is not what I wanted it to be. My belly was bulging, my butt cheeks were larger than I wanted them to be relative to my hips and my hips, yes, my hips, they were much too wide for my liking. I decided to put my bathrobe on so I wouldn't have to see so much of me.

That fall, the weather was warmer than usual. The summer was late leaving and so the plants kept on growing. In the garden, we had squash, peppers, herbs, tomatoes and beans growing still. The beets and radishes were still there too and there seemed to be no urgency to remove them from their nurturing plants.

"Let them grow," Grandma urged. "We'll listen to the news each day and if they call for frost, we'll put a cover on them. Each day still brings with it lots of sunshine so all the veggies can grow bigger. No need to end their season too soon."

It seemed to me that we would never get the kitchen free of canning equipment that year because the growing season was so long. Knowing about karma, I decided I was pushing my luck thinking this way so I decided to be thankful instead, thankful for all the crops that were continuing to produce great food. Peppermint was my favourite tea and seeing those plants still growing encouraged me to have a cup of it while I lounged around the house in my robe.

I thought more about taking yoga and Pilate's classes to tone my body. Some days were very difficult for me because I was alone so much and on that particular day, I became quite depressed, finding it difficult to do much of anything. I found it very hard not having either parent with me and while my memories were ever present, they didn't always fill the void. It wasn't the same as having my mother around and I can't quite explain that.

Sipping more peppermint tea, I began to relax and feel rejuvenated and I could see myself healing, meaning I could now start taking care of myself again, getting my own zest for life back. And with that thought, I got dressed and started thinking about preparing the Sunday dinner for my family.

Sunday dinners growing up were special. Having her glass of red wine in a goblet, Grandma made every meal a delicious one. Sunday afternoons were reserved for making bread, soups and drinking red wine. Most Sundays, Grandma made two loaves of fresh bread for the week. She used whole wheat and unbleached flours and fresh wholesome milk and sunflower oil in each of her recipes. Depending on the meal for that evening, she added spices such as rosemary, basil, dried tomatoes or onions to her bread recipes. Each bread dough was rolled in oats and flax seed or sesame seeds just before allowing it to rise for two hours in the warmed oven. Grandma had a special pan just for bread and never used it for anything else. She liked it because the dough never stuck to the sides and the lid allowed the bread to stay warm such that the yeast always made the dough rise. The pan was round and was the perfect depth for a large loaf of bread. Pumpernickel and round in shape, the recipe changed depending on the mood at the time, but the perfection and deliciousness of each recipe never faltered. On occasion, Grandma would make small buns and small round loaves for individual servings that I loved. Watching the yeast soften in the water and sugar mixture was my favourite part. I loved how it foamed and released an aroma that can only be from yeast. It was a bit sour and a bit sweet all at the same time. Once the yeast was softened, Grandma would then add her two kinds of flour, then add milk, oil and salt to make the best bread in the whole world. At the very end, she rolled it on her bread board in a combination of oats, flax seed, and wheat bran to add the crunch and goodness on the surface of the bread.

Out of the oven, it was moist and warm with lots of flavour and when the butter was added, the taste buds were tantalized. To this day, the smell of bread baking gives me the most comforting feeling. I would do almost anything to have that smell in my house every day.

Grandma was resourceful, too. Whenever she made her bread dough and had all the ingredients out, she would make a pizza dough too that could sit for days in the refrigerator. Once Grandma got a freezer, there was no stopping her with the dough she prepared for defrosting during the week making our favourite foods, with pizza being at the top of the list. Grandma only had to add her fresh ingredients and in less than thirty minutes, we had pizza on the table that was hot from the oven and easy to take with us wherever we had to rush off to. It was a fun bedtime snack in front of the TV too, with a glass of cold milk.

"Don't add any hot peppers to mine," I remember my brother yelling from the living room. "They burn when I to go to the bathroom."

"Oh, that's disgusting," I retorted, but that was my brother. He never cared about how he said things. He just wanted people to react to his comments and I fell for it every time. Now I wouldn't though because I know better, but I wish he were here today to say those dreaded things to me again. How I missed those days.

Later, in my growing years, Grandma continued to cook in the kitchen and bake her breads while Grandpa sat on his chair watching golf, tennis or whatever other sport was on TV all the while drinking beer, gin and sometimes whisky. He could be heard over the sports commentator making his own calls and commenting on the events he was watching, even citing player stats. Sunday afternoons were comforting and meant for the family to relax in the coziness of our home. Only what I didn't know then was, Grandpa was slowly killing himself with booze and inactivity.

Grandma sometimes spilled things in the kitchen while preparing meals and that made her have to stop her cooking to clean it up. Today it was oil. Sunflower oil spilled from the countertop landing on the floor and when it hit, the lid snapped off splattering oil everywhere. What I loved about Grandma was her humour and ability to laugh at these things. "Never mind, Dear," she said while bending down to pick up the toppled oil bottle, reaching for her cleaner under the sink. By always keeping a fresh homemade cleaning spray and clean towel handy, Grandma quickly and efficiently wiped the oil from the floor in just seconds. Today and in my own home, I keep the same homemade cleaner under my kitchen sink; a cleaner that smells of lemons, cucumber and tea tree oil. I love the way Grandma had a whole drawer in her kitchen for clean kitchen towels that were used for dishes and quick clean ups. Tea towels were the secret to efficiency in her kitchen. Grandma always had two types of cleaners in her house; one for general clean ups while food was around and one for disinfecting. Both were fresh, healthy, easy to make and worked on all messes.

Home Cleaning and Disinfectant Spray

Instructions

1. In a spray bottle, mix 1 part 99% rubbing alcohol with 1 part water and ½ part lemon juice or vinegar.
2. Add 40-50 drops of Essential oils such as Clove, Lemon, lemongrass, Scotch Pine, Tea Tree, Orange, grapefruit, Cinnamon, Rose Geranium, Wintergreen, Peppermint, Rosemary, Thyme, Eucalyptus, Rosewood, Elemi.

TIPS:

a. Vary the essential oil to the season pleasing the senses. Smell the oil before adding it to ensure your mood is suited to that oil at the time.
b. Some oils mix very well together such as rosemary and peppermint, clove and cinnamon, lemon and lemongrass, Scotch pine and Tea Tree.

c. Rosewood and Elemi are good for Fall time as they have heavier scents.

d. Eucalyptus is especially nice during cold and flu season along with Scotch Pine and Tea Tree.

e. Rose Geranium is great in the spring when the fresh flowers are blooming.

f. Wintergreen, peppermint, clove and cinnamon mixtures are especially pleasant during the Thanksgiving and Christmas seasons.

General Cleaner

Use recipe for disinfectant cleaner as above, omitting the rubbing alcohol.

Strong Disinfectant Spray

Pour 99% Rubbing Alcohol into a spray bottle and add drops of Essential Oil of your choice for scent. Do not mix with water or lemon juice/vinegar.

Fresh Stains on Clothes

Take a piece of cut lemon and rub directly onto fabric to remove stain. Wash as soon as reasonably possible.

Caution: Some fabrics may discolour or become damaged by the lemon and so caution is to be exercised. Do not use lemon on fabrics you will be sorry to lose in case the fabric stains from the lemon. I use this method when I know the fabric will be destroyed if the stain has a chance to set in and so I take the risk. This sometimes happens when I am eating out.

17

HONESTY

"If you do not tell the truth about yourself you cannot tell it about other people."
-- Virginia Woolf

Standing at the sink, Grandma poured dish soap into the sink making white foamy bubbles that reminded me of the bubble baths I took as a child. Grandma's dish soap always smelled great. It was never a store bought brand, but rather a homemade concoction of liquid castile soap mixed with one of her favourite scents of essential oils. Today it was pink grapefruit, known by Grandma to be a spiritual uplifter relieving exhaustion and muscle fatigue and stiffness. Grandma said she hated washing and drying dishes the most and always wished she could have had a dishwasher. About ten years ago, she bought one but still insists on washing dishes by hand most of the time. I think it's because she likes the smell of her dish soap, but she said it's because she likes to keep her hands busy. Go figure.

"How was your day at work?" she kindly asked me again, as Grandma often did. I was walking into her kitchen surveying the stove and counter looking for what was for dinner.

I let out a small groan and said, "horrid," but chuckled after I said it. I realized how silly it sounded but I couldn't help thinking it. Even though I know I have a good job compared to some, have good working conditions and work fairly close to where I now live so I don't have a long commute, I feel I could be doing better. I could be offering more of my skills elsewhere, learning more and getting paid better. In the company where I work, everyone earns a different wage even if they're doing the exact same job. Where you are on the pay scale depends on how good of a contract you can negotiate for yourself, and negotiating wages required a skill set I don't believe I have.

Grandma never complained about not earning enough money, but I sure do. Grandma would give the shirt off her back to someone who said they liked it. She would literally take it off and say, 'here, please have it, I have another one just like it.' She said that even if it weren't true, but she couldn't stand it if someone poor had no untorn shirt to wear. The first time I saw her do this was also the first time I saw my grandmother in her bra. I remember it was white and large, large all around her upper body. Her chest and her belly were large too, but Grandma wasn't shy. She said she had given birth to children, and this belly was well earned. Her breasts were beautiful and had no doubt been used to feed all her babies. I had heard Grandma was a real beauty in her time but all I saw was Grandma's inner beauty. She could light up the room with her smile, but only when she worked at it. Most of the time, she was very quiet and not really noticeable, taking her place in the background working at serving drinks, food or helping people with their problems and generally making everything comfortable for others to enjoy. Grandma was caring and giving. Probably the most selfless person I knew and she often looked for the natural way to make people feel good.

"What went on today?" she probed.

"Today, the project deadline was missed and my boss was upset and the people who work for me completing the project were either off sick, away on vacation or gearing up to go on vacation. I built in buffer time on the project so nothing's really jeopardized, but it does mean I have to keep my eye closely on it and keep it on my radar all summer long, when I was hoping it would have been done by now so everyone could have an enjoyable summer and not be bogged down by excessive work. Missing this project deadline now means we all have to work hard all summer long and that's going to be very difficult on us because next fall is going to be even busier and we won't be completely rested for it. I'm really sure that people don't think about things like that when they prolong their work thinking and knowing they can drag it out. I mean, there was absolutely no reason for them to have missed this date but rather than all working together to achieve it, they went off individually doing their own thing so now it's not done. With it not being done, it escalated to my level and I have to monitor the project more closely. More work for me and given I don't have any time off this summer, it all amounts to it's just no darn fun, if you get what I mean. On top of all that, they ran to my peer manager and he interfered saying they don't have to do it, meaning the quality of the project will deteriorate. He didn't care about the results and so he pulled them off the project to work on his own and by offering them overtime and extended paid hours, and other private offers, he got them to jump at it. It now means my project will be even further behind. When I asked around to find out why they were pulled to the other project, the answer I got from the manager was that he needed them to work for him and his work was the priority. Then I discovered, they weren't really needed at all. I learned it was a scam, and Grandma, I'm scared. I have reason to believe he's fixing the books. Going through this now reminded me of the time when I first started working with that manager and he told me that his job was to get everyone as much money as he could, and so he made up work that didn't exist or need doing just so he could charge overtime. He was looking to buy me, but I didn't take the bait and I'm glad I didn't either. It would have been like selling my soul to the devil."

"Yeah, I get what you mean," Grandma consoled me. "A similar thing happened to me at the hospital one year and it really took a lot of my energy to set things straight, both with my manager and the other nurses. Sometimes, I don't think people fully understand the impact they have on other people's lives or they don't care. When selfishness sets in, it has effects everywhere and many people suffer because of it. It usually takes a person with a lot of energy and talent to stop the wave of selfishness and turn it around for all to benefit from. But once done, a release of energy in the work force can happen and wonderful things begin to take place. People start to feel good about coming to work and contributing, but not until the selfish ones are removed from the team."

"What happened at the hospital?" I inquired.

Grandma stopped and looked at me as though I had asked her the most intense question. Reaching far into her memory, Grandma began with, "He could charm the snake away from the snake charmer, that's how well he talked up a story. He could spin the finest cloth from the threads of lies and deceit and no one would notice because they were so selfishly drunk with his charm and so fully clothed with the coat of lies he had spun for them, they hadn't noticed the coat was full of moths and in no time at all, their preciously woven coat would be full of holes, eaten by those very moths until nothing but dust was left!"

Wow, I was stunned. I had never heard Grandma talk with such disdain. And then I thought about that time when I saw those freshly picked yellow gladiolas in the vase on her kitchen table. The time when she had makeup on and was cooking a meal and I knew now that Grandma had invited that man to her dinner table that one evening. But would Grandma have invited him into her bed, I wondered? And then I thought about that and realized there was no way she would have. There must have been another reason he was there. Money, perhaps. I knew Grandma had been having a hard time paying her bills and her house was falling into disrepair needing maintenance that Grandpa wasn't doing. Grandpa was never around long enough anymore to care about doing any chores or maintenance on the house and it fell to Grandma to take care of. This is how it had been once Grandpa lost his job. And then I knew it, Grandma was asking that same man for another job and was trying to do it the only way she knew how; by cooking him a good meal. There would have been no affair, at least not in Grandma's plan.

"He eventually moved on to manage a nursing home," Grandma continued, "but while he was at the hospital, he created an environment of delusion leading the department to pick up the pieces after he left. Hospital beds were no longer available because he depleted the funding in the department by constantly overspending while he was the manager. People who were really sick could no longer get the care they so greatly needed. Nurses retired because they couldn't adapt to the lack of quality care being given to the patients. And then some were used to living above their regular wages having become accustomed to the luxury living of the overtime and bonus money they had been given. They selfishly insisted on more money, more benefits and when the hospital board could no longer agree or afford to pay so much, some workers up and left. But God has a great way of turning the bad into good. When the greedy people left, in came a more productive and helpful group of nurses, the kind who genuinely cared for the patients and who were well appreciated for their skills and who appreciated having the job. It turned out well in this case, but the entire time leading to his removal was very uncomfortable for me to be at work. It was difficult knowing we are here to serve, yet watching this nonsense going on thinking God should be stopping this. I kept thinking that with free will, God was planting me there to do His work, to be His example. I kept my head down and continued on with my work as I had always done, but I sure didn't like it. The really bad part was, this person made a lot of money doing this and then went on to another organization doing the same harmful and damaging thing, only under a different job title."

"Oh," I sighed, "you do understand what I'm experiencing."

"Yes, I do, and I'm so sorry this is happening to you. I can only think that while you chose to be where you are, God can use you there to do His work. So listen up, girl, 'cause God's talking to you and He wants to use you to help heal His people. The one sure thing you can do that's in your control is to pray. I once heard a sermon where the clergyman said that if you don't like your minister then pray for the one you have. That made a lot of sense to me because praying helps make us all a better person. That can apply to anyone in your life including your coworkers, parents, teachers or anyone who you don't have control over being in your life. Only your friends, can you choose.

So carrying on with my experience," Grandma continued, "I arranged a meeting to ask this man at the hospital what he was he doing and why he was doing it, thinking I could help to change his thinking, but it was no use. He merely shrugged his shoulders, held open the door for me to exit through and then told me to mind my own business. Well I was indignant, I can tell you, because I thought that was my business." And then, in a quiet voice, Grandma stated, "and I ended up working for him again." Her stare had moved toward the kitchen window.

Looking out the open kitchen window, I saw the sun had come out from behind the clouds and the temperature outside was getting warmer. I liked it when it was hot, just as Grandma did because we could sit by the running stream enjoying the cool fresh water without being chilled. I also liked it because I knew our plants were growing, because they too liked it hot. I thought I'd go for a swim in the creek before dinner and say a prayer while I was out there.

Liquid Dish soap

Instructions

1. Mix together, 1 litre of unscented castile soap with 1-2 tbsp essential oil of your choice (begin with 1 tbsp and adjust to preference).

2. Suggested oils: Lemon, Lemongrass, Tea Tree, Lavender, Scotch Pine, Grapefruit, Orange, Peppermint and Rosemary, Anise Star, Ylang-ylang, Clary Sage and Thyme, Myrrh, and Rose Geranium.

18

THE UNSOLVED HEART

"Have patience with everything that remains unsolved in your heart."
-- Rainer Maria Rilke

This was the day that was filled with heavy heartedness. The weather was cool outside as the earth prepared itself for winter by turning the leaves a brilliant colour of orange, brown, and yellow. The sun was shining, the sky was a light clear blue and the wind was very breezy. It wasn't beach weather but something compelled me to travel there anyway.

Walking along the shoreline with the waves rolling in carrying seed weed and sand, I saw the seagulls hovering above and swooping into shore capturing the food the lake had washed up. Flying high and soaring, they called out warning each other to stay away or to come hither. I didn't understand how birds flocked together and what the dynamics were, but I did know they seemed to understand one another. They appeared to predict each other's flight patterns and graceful swoops into the lake and then back up into the sky, and they didn't seem to crash into each other in spite of their close proximity. And yet, we humans crashed into each other all the time. Cars stopped at intersections and rear ended one another for no apparent reason, or cars T-boned other cars. Or pedestrians were hit while walking on the side walk and cyclists hit on the side of the road. And yet, I've never seen a bird collide with another bird. Oh sure, it may have happened somewhere at some time but I have never seen it or been affected by it.

I had a memory I wished would stop playing in my head. I couldn't help it. It was like I had no way of distracting my mind from replaying the horrid scene over and over again. Meditation, prayer, sports, work, these were all things I used to distract myself from the horrors of the world, but these days, nothing could stop me from repeatedly reliving the collision. The collision that led to the phone call I received while in my kitchen that day I intended to help Grandma with canning the rhubarb and honey syrup jam.

After I had returned from walking on the beach, I looked around my house and saw that I'd been neglecting it. Probably because of the slump I was in.

"You've been living well in this house, Dear," is what Grandma had said. "A house well used is a blessing and God will love that you're living in the house he has blessed you with. Yes, you worked to pay for it, but it was with God's help that you had that job, otherwise, none of this would come to be. Always remember that He blessed you with it and then you will enjoy what you have."

But I know I have to clean it and sometimes I need help, so today, I called the cleaning lady and booked a cleaning. I couldn't have made it without the cleaner's help because sometimes I slipped into a mood where I couldn't function well and didn't want to attend to any of my normal duties and on this particular day, I was remembering the day the crash happened; the crash that stole my great aunt's life, just wrenching my heart out. Losing someone you love by natural causes is hard enough, but losing them by accident is the worse pain I have ever felt. The crash happened on that particular day I got the dreaded phone call.

Grandma didn't have a car of her own and so relied on the goodness of others for getting around. On that particular day, Grandma had been a passenger in the Oldsmobile with her sister Agatha. Great Aunt Agatha was driving and was enjoying the time she had with her sister as these occasions together were getting rarer by time. But while travelling along the dimly lit highway, a car in the oncoming lane attempted to pass the large van in front of it. Pulling slightly into the lane beside it to look around the van, the car's front end immediately hit my great aunt's car sending it flying into the ditch where the rescue workers took several hours getting the two of them out, all the while they laid there unconscious and severely bleeding. That was the day I thought my grandmother was going to die. That was the day my great aunt Agatha did die.

Grandma was gifted with her life back and after eight patient months in the hospital, she slowly recovered and was able to return to her home, for which, we were thankful.

19

FRIENDS IN THE PUMPKIN PATCH

"Only the knife knows what goes on in the heart of a pumpkin."
-- Simone Schwarz-Bart

Halloween was Tabatha's birthday and I believe being born on that day led to her name. We liked teasing her that she looked and acted like a witch but in reality, she was the prettiest girl in class. In fact, she was the prettiest girl I had ever seen. She had amazingly dark brown eyes that were wide open and bright and her shiny dark brown hair was long and straight, perfectly smooth like silk. She was so pretty to me she hardly looked real. Her skin was soft and just the perfect shade of natural beige and her height perfectly complimented her long torso and beautiful legs. I was sure she could be a model in a few years, being only twelve years old now. But Tabatha had a nasty personality, and that changed the way people saw her. I felt sorry for her at first, but once Tabatha sharpened her tongue against me one day, I left her alone to do her own thing. Actually, I was scared of Tabatha because it seemed like she had powers that I couldn't understand, powers to influence people, making them do what I thought were stupid things, like bullying the new kid at school, or making a younger child on the playground cry by taking her ball from her. I always thought Tabatha was a bit mean, but there was one day that I remember clearly when Tabatha and I had a great time together in the pumpkin patch.

It was a cool fall day in mid October and Tabatha and I were playing on a farm in a town called Fenwick. Fenwick is where Tabatha lived and she had invited me to spend the weekend with her. Because she was so pretty and I wasn't, I was in awe that she had invited me to stay with her and I gladly accepted the invitation wondering how I was going to convince my parents to let me spend the weekend away. I'm not sure why, but my parents readily agreed and so Friday after school, I followed Tabatha home taking the same bus as she did while carrying my sleeping bag and overnight clothes case, stowing them under the seat in front of me where we sat on the bus.

The kids on this bus were all different from the ones I knew on my bus, but they behaved much the same way with the cool ones sitting at the back, the quieter, nerdy types sitting in the front and everyone else somewhere in between. I liked to sit in the seat that had the back of the wheel base sticking up so I could I put my feet on it while I sat next to the window and watched what we drove by. Tabatha liked to sit at the back of the bus, in the very last seat and since I had my sleeping bag and carry case with me that wouldn't go under the seat with the wheel base, I decided it was best to sit where Tabatha sat, making myself feel like I belonged with her and the other cool kids. I have to say, it was fun sitting in the very back because I could see all the way up to the front of the bus seeing what everyone was doing and who was sitting with whom or who was talking. I could even hear most of the conversations from where I was sitting because the kids gathered into groups facing backwards to chat. I wasn't used to so much conversation on the ride home, but today it was fun. I sat next to the window in the back and Tabatha sat on the aisle seat where she could spin sideways, putting her feet in the aisle while laughing and chatting with the kids on the other side of the bus. Mostly, I watched and listened thinking this was what it was like to be a cool kid, something I was never considered to be. Slouching down, I put my knees on the back of the seat in front of me and I took in all the sights and sounds waiting for Tabatha's stop to arrive where we would get off at her farm house and walk up the long winding driveway to the white sided house.

Tabatha lived on a pig farm and so the smell took some getting used to, but quickly my nose adjusted to the new smells and my ears heard the noises and grunts from the pigs. Pigs were such interesting animals but I had never been this close to so many of them before. They gathered in groups, just like the kids on the bus and in the school yard, and the pigs oinked at each other, sticking their noses in the air as though they were smelling the air and talking to each other at the same time. It was a real conversation they were having with each other, watching Tabatha and I walk up the driveway with her sisters.

"Emma, they know you're new here and they want to smell you," Tabatha kidded with me.

"Really, they want to smell me?"

Tabatha laughed at me saying, "Gotcha, how would I know if they want to smell you, or if they even can, they're so dirty and smelly themselves."

She was right, they did stink and there was mud all over them, mud from the ground they rolled in and the muddy pond that was inside their fenced in area. But they did seem to notice I was there and a few of them came to the white fence sticking their heads through it as though to say hi to me. Did they want me to pet them? I wondered. And just then, I thought about what we were going to have for supper.

"Come along," Tabatha called out to me. She had gotten ahead of me as

I slowed by the pigs watching them in all their activity. "Come into the house to change our clothes before we go out to the pumpkin patch to play."

Wow, a whole pumpkin patch, I thought. Grandma had a few pumpkins in her garden but never a whole patch on a farm. This surely was going to be interesting to see so many pumpkins all in one place.

After changing our clothes and drinking a glass of milk, Tabatha and I went into the backyard finding a trail leading behind the pig barn and opening up into a huge pumpkin patch. On the far left, corn stalks were growing but Tabatha said that corn was feed for the pigs and not the kind we would eat. She said that was the second crop grown that year and soon, her Dad would take the big machine into the corn field to chop down the stalks feeding the corn into a hopper to store for the winter in the big grain silos. This was so much more than I had ever seen at Grandma's and I knew from what I saw that Tabatha lived on a real farm where her family earned their living from it.

Standing in the pumpkin patch, I looked at all the orange balls of odd shapes around me and saw that some of them were really large while others were quite small. Some had holes in them where I could see the soft orange flesh and slimy seeds inside.

"The bugs and wild animals get to the pumpkins and destroy some by eating them," Tabatha started telling me. "My dad tries to keep the animals away with scare crows and loud air blasting guns, but sometimes the animals are too hungry and come anyway. They like to eat the pumpkins which upsets my father because he sells the pumpkins and only pumpkins that are in good condition can go to market."

This was all brand new to me, and while taking it all in, I began thinking of my grandmother's homemade pumpkin pie. I sure hoped Tabatha's mother was making pie for dessert tonight.

After an hour of playing in the pumpkin patch, Tabatha's sister called us in to wash for dinner and so we left our play area to enter the big farm house and have supper together with the family.

The kitchen in the house was the first room we entered through the back door after we left our muddy shoes in the closed in porch area. There was a large stove that looked like it burned propane, having seen the huge propane tank outside in the yard next to the house when we were playing. The oven, or should I say ovens were stacked in a tower alongside the stove and were white in colour that had faded to a yellow. There were four doors on the oven and I gasped at how large it was.

Tabatha's mother heard me gasp and turned to look at me saying, "are you looking at the stove, Emma? That's on odd thing for a young girl your age to notice."

"Oh," I said surprised that she had taken notice. "I have an easy bake oven and this oven is way bigger than my grandmother's. What are all these doors for?" I asked.

"The bottom door is the broiler where I prepare meats, the middle two are basic ovens, just two in a row as we have a large family and I cook for the farm hands in the field, so I need the two ovens for baking and roasting. The forth door, on the top, is a warming oven where I keep the cooked food warm and warm the bread. I make my own bread, muffins, pies and cakes and so the ovens are quite well used from day to day."

Tabatha's mom seemed like a professional cook to me with her looks and her actions. She wore a full length white apron, tied at her waist and had her hair pinned and tucked up into a net. On her hands, she wore large oven mitts and carefully moved trays and pans of food from the stove to the oven to the counters.

Looking at the table in the kitchen, I wondered where everyone was going to sit, but then I noticed another room with a long table set with dinner plates, knives, forks, spoons, napkins and a table cloth. There was a large light hanging from the ceiling in the center of the table and the glass hanging from it shone like crystals. I will have to ask Tabatha if those are real crystals.

Once our hands and faces were washed in the bathroom, we sat down at the dining room table and Tabatha's father said a prayer of blessing over the food. When the prayer was finished, Tabatha's mom got up from the table, along with her oldest daughter and together they went into the kitchen to carry in the caldron of soup and bread. We each passed our bowls to the head of the table where Tabatha's father and mother began dishing out the soup while Tabatha's sister sliced the bread and passed it around the table for each of us to have a piece. The soup was beef barley with some carrots, celery and onions in it and it was tasty and just the way I liked it. I saw a beef bone in my soup and decided Tabatha's mother cooked the same way my grandmother did, with soup bones, fresh meats and garden vegetables. Did Tabatha know how to cook, I wondered? I doubted so with all those sisters she probably didn't go near the kitchen.

After soup, came boiled Brussels sprouts, carrots, potatoes and here it comes, the platter of meat, wait for it, beef. It was beef and I was so relieved. But where did the beef come from, I thought for only a brief moment before I decided I didn't want to know. And so I ate happily with Tabatha's family, all the while everyone was chatting and talking about the past week and the weekend to come and I really enjoyed myself. Dessert was pumpkin pie, just like I had hoped for and it was delicious too, but by this time, I wasn't surprised because everything on the table had tasted really good.

After dinner, Tabatha and I carried our plates to the kitchen where we left them on the counter and then Tabatha encouraged me to follow her upstairs to her bedroom where she had some comics and reading books to show me. It seemed like Tabatha wasn't expected to do any chores around the house and that was odd to me as I had been raised to help out with everything, but I followed her to her room, feeling only a little bit guilty about leaving the mess for others to clean up. Actually, it felt very weird for me to not be part of the group who works together to clean up. I thought about what conversations and stories I would miss out on by not being with them in the kitchen and it felt lonely to me to not be a part of the family. But Tabatha's dad retreated to the living room where he turned on the TV to watch the news and so I didn't feel quite so different. Tabatha must be like her dad, I thought.

Tabatha's room was small with slanted ceilings and a tall doorway, and it was located on the third floor of the farm house. It was plain but the bed spread had soft pink flowers that I immediately fell in love with, they were so soft and delicate looking. The window coverings were a soft white lace meant only to shield the sunlight from coming into the room. The view outside was of the trees and so no one could look into Tabatha's bedroom window, although I did notice there was a night shade rolled up underneath the top sill.

Tabatha seemed genuinely friendly enough and quiet amongst her family and so I wondered why she was so mean and loud at school and why she treated people the way she did.

"You seem different at home, Tabatha," I commented.

"How so?" she asked.

"I don't know. It's just that, at school, you talk a lot. You also call people bad names and you hang out with only your three friends not letting anyone else play with you. Why is that?"

"I don't like anyone else," she said matter of fact. "But I like you, only you like everyone else and so I can't have you in my group because you'd bring them with you. That's why I asked you here this weekend, so you and

I could play together without everyone else around."

It was odd, but I actually understood what she was telling me and so I relaxed and really began to enjoy my weekend at Tabatha's thinking that it would be weird on Monday morning when she I wouldn't hang out together, but that we would go back to our own friends and continue on the way we had been before.

That night, I dreamt of the great pumpkin patch that we had spent the hour playing in and imagined the pumpkins turning into faces of people who liked me.

Homemade No Crust Pumpkin Pie

This pie has no crust, but forms its own thick texture tasting like filling only.

Ingredients

4 tbsp butter

¾ cup brown sugar

2 eggs

1 large previously baked and mashed butternut squash or 1 medium size pie pumpkin

½ cup whole wheat or unbleached flour

1/8 cup bran flakes

1 cup milk, whole or evaporated

1 tbsp real vanilla extract

1 tsp baking powder

¼ tsp salt

1 tsp ground cinnamon

1 tsp ground allspice

½ tsp ground ginger

½ tsp ground nutmeg

Instructions

1. Preheat oven to 340 degrees Fahrenheit.

2. Blend all the ingredients together in a mixing bowl using a hand held mixer or mixing machine. When thoroughly mixed, pour into an oiled 9 inch deep dish pie tin.

3. Bake 45-50 minutes or until center is cooked as determined by pushing a toothpick into the center of the filling to see if any filling sticks to the toothpick. When filling doesn't stick, the pie is cooked.

4. Place pie on cooling rack and serve chilled. Best to make several hours in advance of serving to allow time for the pie to fully chill.

Variation

Use any mashed fruit or soft vegetable as desired such as zucchini, strawberries and apples, but ensure the consistency is not watery by adding additional flour and sugar. Adding too many eggs will give the pie an omelette taste, similar to that of quiche, but not desirable in a pie.

Basic Pumpkin Spice

Grandma taught me that the flavour we associate with Pumpkin Pie comes from the spices we use. Here is what she used to make her recipes have the pumpkin pie 'taste'.

1 tsp ground cinnamon

1 tsp ground allspice

½ tsp ground ginger

½ tsp ground nutmeg

Mix together and adjust the quantity of each ingredient to please your own taste buds. Add to any baking recipe to make the pumpkin taste come alive.

Pumpkin Pancakes

Ingredients

1 cup whole wheat flour

1/8 cup bran flakes

1 cup milk or plain yogurt or buttermilk

1 egg

2 tbsp butter

¼ tsp salt

¼ tsp baking soda

1 cup of puree which is about ½ small cooked and mashed butternut squash or pie pumpkin

1 tsp ground cinnamon

1 tsp ground allspice

½ tsp ground ginger

½ tsp ground nutmeg

Instructions

1. Mix all ingredients together to form a batter.

2. Ladle 1 cup of batter onto heated grilling pan on medium heat, flipping once bubbles form on the top layer.

3. Serve with fresh fruit and honey or maple syrup.

Variation

Change the flavour of the pancakes by changing what spices are added. The basic pumpkin spices can be omitted and the pancakes will taste just as delicious.

Beef Barley Soup

Ingredients

8-10 large beef soup bones

10-12 cups of water

1 cup pot barley, well rinsed

1 lb stewing beef finely cut

4 medium carrots, diced into bite sized chunks

1 large onion, cooking or Spanish, diced into bite sized chunks

3 stocks of celery, diced into bite sized chunks

1 clove garlic (optional), finely chopped

1/8 cup sunflower oil, can be any light tasting oil such as canola

2-3 tbsp salt and 1tbsp black pepper

Instructions

1. This soup takes all day to make or can be prepared over two days.

2. In a large soup pot or a large slow cooker, place the water, salt, onions, garlic (optional), barley and the beef soup bones in the water bringing to a slow boil.

3. Once boiling, reduce to a simmer and allow simmering for 4 to 6 hours. If using a slow cooker, place cooker on high heat for 4 to 6 hours or low heat for 8-10 hours.

4. This pot can simmer for up to 10 hours, allow to cool overnight.

5. Next day, remove the soup bones and cut off any remaining beef to add back to the soup, discarding the bones.

6. Place soup pot back on medium heat, or high heat for a slow cooker.

7. Add the diced stewing beef, carrots and celery to the pot and allow cooking for 2 to 4 hours until the vegetables and beef are soft and tender.

8. Add pepper to taste either in the pot or in the bowl.

9. Serve hot with fresh rolls or rye toast.

20

NEVER WASTING

"The whole secret of the study of nature lies in learning how to use one's eyes..."
-- George Sand

My grandmother was awesome at using all her food for something. She could turn a meal of left overs into an original meal that was both delicious and visually appetizing. Being with her was one of my greatest pleasures and pass times. She was in awe of her plants and loved the way they constantly gave her food and then more food. "I pick their fruit and they grow more for me," she marveled, "zucchini, radishes, peas, beans, cucumbers, peppers, both sweet and hot, broccoli and tomatoes. They keep on growing!".

Grandma liked picking the peas out of every pod and then drying the pods, grinding them and adding them to what I liked to call, her magic spice jar. There wasn't actually anything magical about the jar, but it was different. No one else I knew made their own spices. I think Grandma invented the veggie spice. She dried a variety of her vegetables, especially peppers that she couldn't eat fresh, included herbs and the leaves from the vegetable plants, ground them up and then mixed them together in one giant jar, inserting a soda cracker into the jar to keep moisture from ruining her powder mix. She used this mixture in all her salads, meats and dishes for the whole year. Grandma rarely cooked with salt and now that I think about it, she didn't need to. Her veggie spice gave her all the sodium she needed for a healthy diet and good nutrition.

The radishes and zucchini gave her vitamin C, the peas and beans gave her protein, B vitamins and vitamin K and the cucumbers gave her folic acid, while the peppers gave her carbohydrates, more vitamins C, K, and B6, beta-carotene, thiamine and lots of fiber. The tomatoes gave her sodium and the broccoli gave her most of the benefits as the peppers, but additionally protected her from cancers. That's what Grandma believed.

"Do you know why I can see so well and at my age too?" Grandma asked me.

"No, Grandma, tell me the story again," I replied every time.

"It's because I eat my veggies. My peppers, Granddaughter, are like magic. When all my friends got cataracts, they laughed at me when I told them I wouldn't be getting those, and all because I eat my peppers. You see, peppers have so much vitamin C and beta-carotene in them, they help to protect my eyesight."

While my friends talk about these things now, in my grandma's day, this was witch craft. How could a plant prevent cataracts?

"How do you know this, Grandma?" I asked.

"I know this because the plants tell me. I listen to my plants, and they talk to me because I'm sensitive and I listen. Whenever I eat something from the garden, I feel so great and healthy. I wait to see what starts to feel better first and whenever I eat peppers, my breathe freshens up and my eyesight gets clearer. And that, my lovely granddaughter, is how I know. That's how it works for me."

Grandma's spice jar was a work of art and each year I looked forward to helping her pick the vegetables, wash them, dehydrate them and then grind them into fine powder. When it was all mixed together, the spice jar was an earthy green and brown colour and so sometimes Grandma separated it into smaller batches adding paprika to one batch making it red and then parsley to another batch making that one green in colour. In doing this, she had an instant and nutritious way of fancying up her dishes by sprinkling them with herbs. Green and red livened up many meals.

The Spice Jar

Instructions

1. Dehydrate Vegetables and Herbs (suggestions below).
2. Grind up in blender, food processor or coffee grinder.
3. Mix all together and store in a an air tight container.

TIP:

Keep hot chili peppers in a separate glass jar.

Suggested foods for dehydrating:

Peppers of all varieties including red hot chili peppers (but keep these separate), Broccoli – leaves, sprouts and heads, Peas, Beans, Carrot tops (greens), Tomatoes, Zucchini, Cucumber, Rosemary, Thyme, Parsley, Sage, Basil, Leeks, Green onions, Chives, Oregano, Celery

21

OATMEAL

"You have to eat oatmeal or you'll dry up. Anybody knows that."
-- Kay Thompson

The Prairies are a spectacular sight for growing wheat and oats and if you've ever been out there you would first notice the vast amount of land with its miles and miles of flat farms where wheat grows annually. Driving across the Trans Canada highway as a young child with my family, we saw wheat silos off in the distance that took us over an hour to drive to. This was in such contrast to Ontario where the trees bordered the roads and the view was kept narrowed by the tree line.

Driving through Manitoba and Saskatchewan with Grandma in the back seat with me and the family dog on the seat between us, Grandma and I were captured by the tranquility of the land and the view of the brown wheat growing all around us.

"Emma, the farmers here in the Prairies grow wheat as their main income and most of the world eats either wheat, rice or potatoes. Wheat is one of the world's most common crops and is very nutritious if left unrefined as it has germ and bran in it which is great for supplying vitamins E, B1, B2, B3, B5, B6 and folic acid to the body," Grandma educated me.

"What does being left unrefined mean?" I asked.

"It means it hasn't been through a process where the bran and germ have been removed from the plant and sold off for other food items to make a further profit. It means the wheat hasn't been bleached to make it white in colour or increased in gluten which is a tough substance for the body to digest. If left in its whole form, the wheat can help the body to fight diseases especially in the stomach and colon area," Grandma explained.

Most of what Grandma talked about was way beyond what I could understand, but I loved hearing her talk passionately about the food and the wheat that grew around us and so I listened attentively, enjoying her attention on me and I did learn things from her that I remembered into my adult life, things like, eat whole wheat flour, and not refined white flour.

Oats were another crop that were grown in the Prairies, and so along with eating whole wheat, my grandmother indulged in oats, just like the farm animals and just like the lamb I had seen at my friend's house. Well, not quite just like, but close enough. When Grandma was hungry on a cold winter day, she ate oatmeal and she ate it with real maple syrup and cinnamon with butter and raisins too. I hated oatmeal when I ate it at home because my parents used artificial syrup and margarine, but then Grandma made it for me and I loved it. Grandma made it with real ingredients and none of that processed stuff that's too quick to cook and ready in just a few minutes. She used real maple syrup and butter. My taste buds could tell the difference and I noticed that Grandma could make her oatmeal in just the time it took me to change from my pyjamas and come to the breakfast table. She made rye or whole wheat toast with it and it was all so delicious I could eat a whole bowl full, all by myself.

I sat with my grandmother one morning eating an oatmeal breakfast at her large oak table, when she began telling me about the goodness of oatmeal and all the health benefits of it such as its high content of bran, germ and fibre and it was such a familiar story after hearing her talk about the wheat, I thought I must have memorized the ingredients. Only oats seemed to be a little bit different than wheat.

"Oats have minerals in them, Emma, minerals that the body needs to stay healthy with such as iron and magnesium and vitamin B which is good for converting the food you eat into fuel that your body can use as energy. Oats are good for your blood too and keep your heart healthy which, in itself, is worth eating them." She explained that oats helped in weight loss diets because the body burned energy digesting them.

And so, I put oats in my breakfast foods including pancakes, bread, cereal and potato pancakes. And whenever I make smoothies in the blender, oats find their way into those too. Later in life, flying over the Prairies reminded me of Grandma and her philosophy on wheat. Oats and wheat are grown in abundance in Canada's Midwest provinces and Grandma's homemade breads came to my mind each time I looked down from the skies through the plane's window as I flew over the vast fields that would feed millions of people each year. Wheat is to eat, I humoured myself with.

Pancakes

Ingredients
Flour, unbleached or whole wheat (same recipe)
Water
Egg
Salt
Sunflower or Almond Oil

<u>TIP:</u>

To avoid a mess on the stove and countertop, pour pancake batter using a funnel into an empty ketchup bottle and tipping upside down, squeeze the pancake batter into the pan.

Whole Wheat Potato Pancakes with Oats

Ingredients

1 small onion, peeled and grated
1 medium potato, well scrubbed and grated
½ cup whole wheat flour
¼ cups rolled oats
Salt and Pepper
Garlic powder (optional)
1 egg, beaten
1/8 cup light tasting cooking oil, such as canola, sunflower, peanut

Instructions

1. Combine all ingredients above except cooking oil, in a bowl and mix together thoroughly.
2. Preheat cooking oil in a non stick pan.
3. When oil is heated, spoon equal parts of mixture into oil, and flatten into a patty being carefully not to be burned by the oil.
4. When browned on bottom, flip patty and cook until brown on the other side.
5. Remove from pan and place on paper towel to drain oil. Serve warm or cold.

Banana Yogurt Smoothie (Blender drink)

Ingredients

1 whole banana, peeled

1 cup of water

1 cup of yogurt of any variety

1/8 cup of oats

1 cup of favourite seasonal fruit (optional)

Instructions

1. Blend together until smooth.

2. Garnish with a piece of pineapple (for digestive enzymes, or parsley for chlorophyll).

Variations

Add any fruit to the above banana smoothie including blueberries, strawberries, apples, peaches, lemons and oranges. If adding lemons or oranges, place the entire fruit in the blender because the peels have bioflavonoids that help with vitamin absorption and utilization.

TIPS:

a. Banana can be removed if preferred.

b. Using a yogurt with Probiotics will give added benefits.

22

THE FRUIT OF MY FOOD

"Eat an apple on going to bed, and you'll keep the doctor from earning his bread." -- Unknown

I would be remiss in my story telling if I didn't tell you about my grandmother's love for both vegetables and fruit and in particular, for apples. An apple a day keeps the doctor away, were words she not only said, but lived by.

My uncle owned a large property in a place called Stoney Creek and way at the back of the land, there grew a single apple tree. It grew the variety of apples called delicious and while these are in general my favourite type of apple, never has the word delicious been more fitting. But at the time of seeing this apple tree, I hadn't eaten one and so I didn't know what treat lay ahead of me as I meandered down the freshly cut lawn toward the back of the property.

It was a beautiful sunny October day and my aunt and uncle were hosting their twentieth wedding anniversary at their country estate. Their estate home had been earned through some smart business ventures and hard work. The family was all there including their own children and extended families and it was great for us to all be together for a happy occasion. After enjoying some casual conversation and some barbequed food, I wandered to the back of the property to have a look around and there I found a lone apple tree, ripe with the apples for picking. Remembering my grandmother's love for apples and hearing her voice in my mind saying, apples have so many good things about them, Emma, they should be eaten every day, I found myself reaching up to grab one from the tree. The vision of Adam and Eve came to me at that time as I reached for the apple and I caught myself wondering if in fact, I should be eating that apple, imaging Eve being tempted by the serpent to eat from the tree of knowledge. "Oh that's silly," I caught myself saying aloud, and I picked the apple with my outreached hand. I checked it for spoiled spots and then rubbed it on my sleeve to remove any dust, polishing it to a shine. I then took a bite, and there it all was... the explosion of flavour, sweet juice, loud crunch, chewy crispness and the delicious taste of apple all in my mouth. This was, perhaps, the tastiest, most sensuous apple I had ever eaten, and I'm so tempted to grow an apple tree in my own back yard so I can have this taste sensation every year. It was a disappointment to me when my aunt and uncle sold the property as I knew I would never have that same experience again. One good thing for me is I'm living near an apple farm where I can buy apples almost as good as the one I had that day.

Apples have the kind of goodness in them that may not all be found in other fruits, goodness such as pectin, vitamin C, flavonoids, antioxidants, phenols, cancer fighting properties, bacteria fighting properties and phytonutrients. And apples can aid in healing respiratory ailments, I've read. Grandma knew from her nursing background how important apples were to helping patients heal and so she ensured she always had a fresh supply in her kitchen.

Grandma's apple pie was killer, meaning it was the best apple pie I've ever eaten, but she didn't limit her inclusion of apples to just pie. No sire, she used apples in muffins, cookies, pancakes, waffles, breads, cobbler, chili, spaghetti sauce, oatmeal and even in stews. No apple ever rotted in her house and no week ever passed by without apples being included in the menu. Had the apple not been discovered, I wonder what my grandmother would have used to sweeten her food with or to add texture and moisture to muffins.

Grandma put love into every meal and that love could be tasted in every bite. Turkey dinners were festive with an apple being baked in the cavity of the turkey instead of stuffing. The apple added a slight sweet flavour to the meat and enhanced the gravy. Watching Grandma prepare a turkey, I was quiet as I observed her start with the stuffing by cutting the French bread into cubes on a cutting board and then browning the cubes on a tray in the oven. While those were browning, Grandma simmered sliced onions, celery and the turkey liver and heart in a saucepan with some salt, pepper, and olive oil. Once the diced bread was removed from the oven and placed in a mixing bowl, Grandma added olive oil to the dried bread to soften the cubes. She added in her dried garden herbs such as rosemary, basil, celery, thyme, sage and parsley and mixed those all into the bread. The olive oil helped the herbs to stick to the bread cubes. When the simmered onion mixture was prepared, she poured the contents of the sauce pan onto the bread cubes and began mixing it together. She tasted it, added a bit more salt and pepper and then just a tad more olive oil and when she was satisfied, she put the bowl aside on the counter.

"What are you going to do with that, Grandma?" I asked.

"Later, after the turkey is cooked, there will be juice in the roasting pan and I'll put a cup or two of that seasoned turkey water into the bowl to soften the stuffing, heating it too. Once the stuffing is moist, I'll place it in the oven to finish warming and then serve it with dinner. In this way, the stuffing will taste like the turkey without having to be cooked inside of it," Grandma explained in her detailed way that she often did when she was teaching me how to cook. "You see, Emma, most people cook their stuffing inside the turkey, but then the turkey is hard to cook and its difficult to gauge when it's done, often leaving the turkey either undercooked and raw near the bone, or over cooked and dry. Eggs are used in stuffing to bind the stuffing together when cooked in the turkey otherwise the stuffing will fall apart because it's too moist. But the eggs take a long time to cook and can't be left raw. To keep from drying the turkey out, people will often cook the turkey on a low temperature and baste it often. Doing all that basting is too fussy for me and it's hard to keep bending over the oven, lifting the turkey in and out and it causes all the heat to escape from the nice warm oven," she went on.

"So how do you cook the turkey?" I ventured to ask.

"Watch and learn," was her answer as she gave me a soft smile, arching her eyes brows in play.

While drinking my glass of milk, I watched as Grandma placed the large roasting pan on the counter and then carefully put dried stems from her garden herbs in the bottom of the pan. Again, she used dried rosemary, sage, parsley, basil, thyme and celery. Once the bottom of the pan was completely covered with what I thought looked like way too many stems, she put the wire lifting rack on top of the herbs. She then took the clean turkey from the sink and placed it on the rack. She stuffed the cavity of the turkey with two apples she had washed and cut in half and then closed the cavity by hooking the turkey legs into the skin that hung there. Grandma then placed ten marrow filled soup bones that had been cut by the butcher into round segments around the edge of the roasting pan, surrounding the turkey. She measured out eight cups of water and poured the water over the turkey and the bones distributing it evenly around the pan. She then sprinkled a bit of rosemary over the turkey along with powdered sage and thyme which stuck to the top.

Holding the lid in her right hand, she took one last long look at the marvelous bird in the roasting pan and I could tell she was quite pleased with her work. Smiling, she covered the pan and placed it in the oven on 350 degrees Fahrenheit. Closing the oven door, she turned to me and said, "And that, Emma, is how you cook a turkey."

I couldn't help but laugh. She was so dramatic in how she expressed her appreciation for beautiful food. And I knew Grandma was grateful for it too.

The turkey was ready in about two and half hours and she only lifted the lid once after about two hours of cooking to check in on it. She said it would be done when it was a golden brown. When the turkey was cooked, Grandma took two cups of the flavourful turkey juice from the pan and added it to the bowl of stuffing, mixing it thoroughly and then placing it in the hot oven. She then made gravy with another two cups of the turkey juice which she referred to as pan drippings. The potatoes were cooked and mashed and the cranberries were chilling in the refrigerator.

When we were ready to eat, the turkey was carved and a prayer of Thanksgiving was said as we counted our blessings for our family, friends and food. Grandma often said, "cooking is a work of art," and I follow her by saying, "cooking is a skill of the craft."

Apple Pie

Pie Crust

Ingredients

2 cups whole wheat flour

1 cup softened butter (not melted)

Up to 1/4 cup lukewarm water

Instructions

1. Combine flour and butter first and then only enough water to make a soft dough ball. Add the water by the tablespoon to ensure the right amount is used.

2. Tip: If too much water has been added, more flour and butter can be added.

3. Split the pastry into two balls and roll each ball out with a rolling pin to make a bottom and top to the pie crust.

4. Place the bottom in a deep dish 9 inch pie plate.

Filling

Ingredients

1 cup brown sugar

¼ cup molasses

¼ cup honey

¼ cup water

1 cup large flake rolled oats

1 tbsp ground cinnamon

6 large apples, washed and sliced from the core (Grandma wasn't particular about which kind of apples she used in her pie, she used whatever she had and she never peeled them)

Instructions

1. Preheat oven to 350 degrees Fahrenheit.

2. In a small sauce pan, combine brown sugar, molasses, honey and water and heat to a gentle rolling boil.

3. Allow to boil for 3-5 minutes and then add cinnamon and oatmeal, removing from heat.

4. Stir and add sliced apples so the apples are coated with the mixture.

5. Add apple mixture to pie crust and cover with dough topping.

6. Place in oven and cook until pie crust is golden brown as desired, about 20-30 minutes.

7. Remove from oven and place on cooling rack.

Apple Crisp

Ingredients

5 washed and sliced apples (skin on)
¼ cup brown sugar
¼ cup honey or maple syrup
2 cups large flake rolled oats
¼ cup raisins
2 tsp ground cinnamon

Instructions

1. In an oven dish or casserole, combine the above ingredients and stir together thoroughly.

2. Place in preheated oven at 340 degrees Fahrenheit for 20 minutes until bubbly hot.

3. Place on cooling rack for 10 minutes and serve warm. This is delicious for breakfast too.

Whole Wheat Apple Muffins with Nuts and Raisins

Ingredients

2 ½ cups Whole Wheat flour
1 cup milk
1 cup brown sugar
½ cup white sugar
1 tsp baking soda

1 tsp baking powder

2 fresh eggs

2 tbsp oil, such as sunflower, canola, vegetable or almond oil

1 cup apple sauce

3 tsp cinnamon

2 tsp allspice

1 tsp salt

1/2 cup mixed chopped nuts and seeds such as walnuts, almonds, peanuts, pine nuts, cashews, pumpkin, sunflower, etc (optional)

½ cup dried fruit such as cranberries or raisins (optional)

2 cupcake baking sheets lined with large cupcake papers

Instructions

1. Preheat oven to 340 degrees Fahrenheit.

2. Combine all the ingredients, except the nuts and raisins, together in a large mixing bowl and blend using a mixer until the mixture is thick enough to stay on a spoon but not so thick as to lump on the spoon. The mixture should be slightly liquid. Add more milk or flour in very small amounts to reach desired thickness. Grandma liked to taste the mixture before using to ensure she liked the flavour before baking. She could then adjust for sugar, salt, oil and spices as desired.

3. Stir in nuts, seeds and raisins at this time, if desired.

4. When satisfied with mixture, ladle into cupcake papers in tray and place in oven for 20 minutes until muffins are firm but soft on top.

5. Remove from oven and allow them to cool before serving. Muffins can be frozen or stored in refrigerator in plastic bags for up to three days.

Variation

Cranberry sauce can be used instead of apple sauce to change the flavour of the muffin to Cranberry Lemon.

Homemade Cranberries

Ingredients

3 cups fresh cranberries, washed

2/3 cup freshly squeezed lemon juice (1 small lemon)

1/3 cup water

¾ cup sugar

Instructions

1. Combine all ingredients in a medium size pot and boil on medium low heat for 20-30 minutes or until the sauce starts to thicken.

2. Place in a serving bowl and chill for about 3 hours before serving.

Variation:

The amount of sugar, lemon juice and water can be adjusted to the desired sweetness and tartness as long as the liquid volume remains the same. More sugar can be added if desired, up to a total of 1 cup.

23

ON PERSONAL ENERGY

"The energy of the mind is the essence of life."
-- Aristotle

"I've always admired your ability to look young and stay active," Abigail said to her sister, Belle, as they strolled down the street. Both sisters had been missing their beloved Agatha and so were trying to spend more time with each other making up for the emptiness they felt, and so they planned for one morning a week to be together to catch up with each other lives. Today, they were window shopping downtown.

"Your skin is fresh and clear and your eyes too, Belle. How do you get that way?"

As pretty as Grandma's name was, Rosa Belle, most preferred to shorten it to Belle.

"It's all that great work I do in the garden every summer," Belle replied to her sister.

"It keeps my circulation going so my whole body gets the oxygen it needs to stay healthy. And then I eat all that great locally grown food that's so fresh, it nourishes my cells keeping them healthy," she said smiling. "You know Abby, I've often wondered why you choose to buy your food from food markets and why now, you're even buying frozen, pre packaged food when you could be eating fresh live food from the garden. Mom would have a heart attack if she were to see what you're eating and doing to yourself. Especially since she taught us all how to cook and we're so creative. We're great cooks."

"Ah, it's not that I don't know how to cook, it's that I don't have time. I get up too early in the morning, get ready for work, spend all day working my butt off and then when I come home, I'm hungry, tired and miserable. I can't get the energy I need to be creative in making a meal, simple or otherwise. All I can think of is eating food, right then and there. So I grab packaged food that I hear only takes minutes to heat and then I'm eating. I know you're right, Mom would have words with me if she were alive today to see this," Abby explained to Belle.

"Everyone talks about work life balance and yet in our society, this is non existent. Everyone is so busy, that no one has time to sit around, just talking and making homemade meals," Belle chimed in.

"Ah, yes," Abby agreed. "It's certainly true that the days are busy and the stresses in life are plentiful. Of course, we've always had stresses in life, but they were different than they are now. Before, it was much too hard to travel or stay in touch with long distance friends and co workers so everything that was done, was done locally. Now we communicate with the whole world in an instant. We have cell phones and internet connections that connect us immediately to anyone, anywhere, and for some people, this gives them an advantage in life because they're connected to their families. For others, it means we're working longer hours, juggling more items and compressing more chores into shorter time frames. For example, years ago when it was bill paying time, I would spend the whole morning organizing the bills, go for a little walk taking my mail to the post office to send off and while I was out, I could gather a few groceries, stop off at the library to get a few good books to read, come home, make lunch and then sit with my book for a couple of hours in the afternoon reading and escaping into my fantasy world of the novel I was reading. My mind was alert, my body was resting during the afternoon lull time and my belly was satiated. And, it was home cooked food I was eating. But today, bill paying is done in the evening on the computer in just fifteen minutes and no energy is spent walking anywhere which means I get no exercise or fresh air out of it, and no stop at the grocery store to inspire home cooking and no good books are borrowed from the library. Instead, I grab a frozen dinner from the freezer, microwave it, turn on the TV, eat, get up to walk to the computer, sit down again, pay the bills, get back up and watch more TV. To do anything else would require energy which I just don't have. It's an endless cycle."

"You know, we've really hit on to something here," Abby continued conversing with her sister. For me, if I want to do something beyond what I budgeted for, the cost is so expensive that I can't do it without working overtime for the money which means I'm away from home even more and working harder. Don't get me wrong, the job I have pay wells enough, but it's for the basics in my life like the house I live in, the clothes I wear and the car I drive. I don't have a big fancy house or car and I don't wear expensive clothes either. In fact, I buy some new clothes to look fashionable in only every few years. Other times I visit the second hand shops and select high quality hand me downs that still have years of wear left in them. They feel new to me and they look good, and I like that I'm supporting the local charities, but honestly, Belle, it would be nice to spend some extra cash on brand new clothes more often than I do. Now back to this energy thing, Belle. To get energy, I have to expend energy, but I don't have spare energy to get going with. How do I get around that?"

"Ginseng," Belle offered.

"Uhh? What on earth is that?" Abby sounded horrified but asked anyway.

"Ginseng. It's a Chinese root and it tastes earthy but delicious at the same time and just maybe, it has that extra burst of energy you're looking for. It can be boiled in water with soup broth, steeped in hot water for tea with added honey for sweetness or it can be eaten as a liquid in a blender drink or as a capsule with a glass of water. Yerba mate and green tea can help with energy too. A touch of caffeine and antioxidants have a great way of hydrating and restoring the body, providing extra boosts of energy."

"Can I add this ginseng to my vegetable juice?" asked Abby.

"Why yes, of course. That's a great thing to do," replied Belle. "Adding it to freshly juiced vegetables will give you even more nutrients which then help the body to repair itself even faster, giving you more energy in a shorter time frame. How clever it is of you to think of that, Abby."

"Well, we are our mother's daughters and Mom was smart. A very mature soul, she was."

Being a naturalist, my great grandmother understood the connection between the mind, body, spirit, nutrition, and energy flow. She understood how our thoughts and our emotions controlled our behaviours and she understood how our overall health was affected by what we thought, how we felt and how we behaved. Today, we know things in North America like Reiki, and how energy flows within the body to reduce stress, promoting relaxation and healing through this life force energy. My great grandmother passed on the wisdom to her family that having high life force energy promoted happiness and overall healthiness. But she was sure to believe that the Holy Spirit was to be the only spirit she would call upon for her soul.

"Along with using Reiki treatments, ginseng root was largely consumed by the Chinese and used for supporting the immune system and energy flow through the body and is used widely in North America today. Some common types of ginseng include Red, Siberian and Korean," Grandma explained.

And so continuing their walk and window shopping together, Belle and Abby chatted and laughed their way through the remainder of the afternoon enjoying each other's company immensely. Afternoon tea was enjoyed back at Grandma's house where she introduced Abby to ginseng, adding some to their green tea with lemon and honey.

24

RETIREMENT

"And in the end it's not the years in your life that count. It's the life in your years." -- Abraham Lincoln

"Don't wait until you retire to have fun," Grandma said to me one morning while we were driving to church.

"What's that, Grandma?" I asked, having not quite heard her because she said this one statement with no context behind it.

"Don't wait until you retire to have fun. It will be too late then and your dreams will have changed. The world will be a different place and the opportunities will have disappeared. Oh, there will still be opportunities, but they'll be different ones. They'll look different and require different things than those you planned for. The opportunities you planned for won't look the way you saw them when you were dreaming about them, only you won't know that until you get there and the magic isn't what you dreamed it would be. The feeling will be different and you won't have control over that."

Looking at Grandma over my right shoulder while I was driving, I tried to catch her eye wondering at the same time what she saw and was referring to and I couldn't help but wonder what dreams she had dreamt at my age, and what dreams had gone unrealized for her due to changing circumstances.

"The billboard we had driven by showed 3 women my age laughing together while holding their hands high in the air, but they're not really feeling that happy," Grandma commented. "Those are actresses pretending to enjoy the moment. But do you see their husbands there with them? No. And that's because they're dead. Their joy is gone, their love is gone and now they're trying to find joy but they don't really feel it. It's not deep down inside like it would be if their men were alive," she carried on.

Thinking Grandma was feeling down, I was glad we were on our way to church because Grandma appreciated God's comfort and always felt brighter after mass. She would call God's name and there He would be, ready with arms wide open to give a hug.

I think Grandma really missed Grandpa, more than she would let on. Grandpa died of liver cancer. As a young child, I remember his character.

"Belle, get the kids ice cream!" he bellowed from his bluish green recliner chair parked in front of the television set watching his favourite programs, including The Lawrence Welk show and sports. By saying kids, he meant Shelby and I. The only place I ever saw Grandpa sit was on that recliner chair. Drinking is what killed him. Drinking alcohol caused his liver cancer. I don't think Grandma ever quite forgave him for that either. There she was always cooking healthy food, growing it in her gardens and there he was out in the bar drinking with his friends or sitting on the chair drinking alone. Grandpa was always loyal to Grandma and never once cheated on her with another woman, but Grandma felt he cheated on her with drink.

"Drank away our golden years, he did." Grandma continued. "He was such a strong, healthy man when I met him and big too, with solid muscles.

That man could lift his own weight and with his strength, he built my gardens just the way I wanted them. He built our home too, a home where we were to raise our family and grow life under its roof and in the yard. And then slowly, little by little, he began eating too much, drinking too much and gaining too much weight. He stopped doing things that gave him exercise and it spiraled downward into darkness. He ate and drank even more then, and moved even less. I kept begging him to change the pattern, but he didn't see it. Or maybe he did, but he didn't acknowledge it, and it kept breaking my heart to see this happening. In the whispering hope of it all, I kept my gardens growing and the goodness harvested thinking he would come around to good health and vitality once again. But it was too late by the time he noticed it. He thought he was invincible and the sorrow that followed has never gone away."

"Love, Grandma."

"What?"

"Love, Grandma."

"Yes, I heard you, Emma, I'm not deaf. But what did you mean by saying that?"

Chuckling a little out loud while still driving, I thought to myself that Grandma was at least partly herself this morning, and that she hadn't completely deserted me.

"What I mean is that love makes the world a better place, and with love in your heart, you can forgive Grandpa for changing your future and your retirement from what you planned it to be. You might even feel joy."

"Hard work is the back bone of our society," Grandma spoke softly. It's true, she was the one who worked so hard in our family. Grandma didn't have the skills of a supervisor or a manager, but she did have the work ethics of someone who knew and appreciated the value of a good day's labour. And for that, we all ate very well and we had clean clothes and a clean house to come home to. But Grandpa, now he was of a different mindset. Grandpa was well liked for his kindness, generosity and his overall pleasantness. At one time, Grandpa had a valuable skill set but he chose not to keep it developed after his company closed. Instead, for him, life became about living in the moment and escaping the long term planning for the future. He squandered away his days and his life in sorrow and pity for himself. He started changing his mindset and he believed in what his negative thoughts were telling him. Why would his grown children need money from him in the future when they could work for it themselves? I was never sure if Grandpa was filled with evil thoughts or if he just had an emotional and mental breakdown after he lost his job, a breakdown that lasted for much of his adult life. Either way, Grandpa was a man who had a wife, children and grandchildren and yet he began ignoring them all. I had no real recollection of what he did most days other than what I saw of him sitting in his recliner chair, but I do remember he had never lived up to Grandma's anticipations. I don't suppose he meant to be that way, only he didn't know how to break the spell.

This glimpse into Grandma and Grandpa inspired me to think of my own life with my own husband, once I was married. I tried to encourage my man to eat healthy and to cook more rather than to eat out. But it began occurring to me then that this healthy lifestyle is my way of life and not his. His life is about takeout food, quick and tasty but filled with chemicals and expensive too. Mine's about no chemicals, food in its simplest and whole form that I can make and food that hasn't been touched or breathed on by too many people. When I bring home the milk and orange juice cartons from the grocery mart, I wipe them down with a damp cloth before I place them in my refrigerator eliminating as many germs as possible. The fruit is washed and placed cleanly in crispers and the left over foods are covered to minimize any dust or particles from settling on them or from depositing odours to other food. Will I still get cancer, I wondered? Maybe. This horrific disease takes the life out of so many people, but not as many as heart disease, I've read, but more painfully it seems. Interestingly enough, I would think the heart should be the one thing we protect as it pumps the oxygen and nutrients in our blood all around our bodies and to all organs.

"Our Father, Who art in Heaven," the congregation began to pray together out load. "...Give us this day our daily bread..." I must remember to bake a loaf of bread when I get home. Two; I'll need two loaves for this week. "...Amen". I was so afraid of having a diseased body my prayers were interrupted thinking how to eat better.

And so Grandma and I enjoyed our hour together at mass before returning home to make the Sunday meal, including freshly baked bread to go with our roast beef dinner.

Roast Beef and Garlic Potatoes with Asparagus and Carrots

Prep time: 10 minutes

Ingredients

1 roast beef of any cut or size
1 cup of water
3 medium onions, peeled
8 large potatoes, or 2 per person, washed (but not peeled)
4 cloves of garlic
4 large carrots
4 spears of asparagus per person

Instructions

1. Place all ingredients except asparagus in slow cooker on low for 6-8 hours.

2. When roast is cooked, steam asparagus above boiling water and serve

together hot.

Variations:

a.   Serve garden salad and soup as appetizers for added nutrition.

b.   Substitute roast for pork or chicken or go vegetarian adding a variety of your favourite vegetables and seasonings.

TIP:

Prepare this meal the evening before putting the uncooked pot in the refrigerator. Next morning, pull it out and start it slowly cooking. Dinner will be ready for you when you return home tired in the evening.

25

FRAGRANCES AND SEXUALITY

"A woman who doesn't wear perfume has no future."
-- Coco Chanel

Growing up, sexuality was always the hot topic. It was cool to be gay, it was cool to do drugs and it was cool to love hard rock and have sex. Generation after generation felt this liberation to express freedom of choice through rock and roll and the bands of the fifties, sixties, seventies, eighties and nineties were the catalysts to many changes in teenager and young adult behaviours. Priorities shifted from working the land to working the bars. Leisure time was in abundant and was used to socially bond with people and explore the most primitive instinct known to man and animal; sex. The mating ritual was no longer about finding the strongest person to build the family with, but instead was about finding the hottest and sexiest person and possibly the most messed up, well at least it seemed like they were the most messed up, but that was hard to define because drugs in itself messed up a person.

The one thing I remember the most from growing up was the smell of things around me. The funny thing about fragrances is that they are a pathway to the memory, and a very powerful one too. I can hear familiar noises or see particular movements in such a way that may remind me of the past and of things I have seen before, but the most prevailing sense to a memory is when I smell something. It's kind of like when I smell baking bread, I think of Grandma's kitchen, or when I smell apple pie baking, I feel the warmth of her kitchen from the oven and I see the familiar and comforting body of my grandmother with her apron tied around her waist stirring the bowl filled with apples, cinnamon and nutmeg knowing that when this is all mixed together and baked, the most delicious taste sensation will be experienced.

As so this is how I relate to my teenage years when I think of bars and the smell of stale beer, and dirty urinals. The dance floor dark with stains and scuffs were barely noticeable the night before, partly because the lights were dimmed too low to see and partly because the floor was too packed with people to see it. Beer and sweet drinks were spilled all night long on the floor and yet the people were having the best times in their lives. Soon they would be grown up with jobs and responsibilities of their own that would have most of them out growing this party atmosphere. They will have found their mates and then moved them on to cleaner and better smelling places. Places that don't smell of sex and raw animal sensuality like the smell of urine, cheap perfume and testosterone combined.

"Fragrances can hold the power in your life because they have the power to alter your mood and your state of health," Grandma told me one day while holding a bottle of her favourite essential oil, lavender. "The power of the fragrance in natural plants and flowers is nourishment and food to the soul and to the organs within the body. God has put all things on this earth that we need to be healthy and vibrant with and essential oils are among those things that God helps to lavish upon us. Once in its oil state, the concentrated form of the plant can increase circulation, boost immune systems, be energizing, uplifting, refreshing, warming and restorative to our body's natural balance keeping us healthy and ready to face the world."

"But Grandma, don't perfumes do that too. I mean, why do the perfume companies make so many different products?" I loved perfumes and how fabulous they smelled and I wanted Grandma to tell me it was alright for me to use them.

"Fragrant oils, Dear, have always been thought of to be harmful to the body and are synthetically produced. But for some reason, people today don't notice the health and state of the body as much as we did when I was growing up. Partly because I think young people of today don't use their bodies to survive in the way I had to growing up, and partly because total health wasn't fully understood either. When my work was hard and physical, I had to be at my healthiest because when I was sick and weak, the work didn't get done, and food wasn't on the table and the shelters weren't built and the livestock weren't cared for. Today, most people don't tend to those chores and therefore don't notice their bodies becoming weak and frail. Many people overeat making the size of their bodies larger, yet unhealthier. Bones are weaker, tendons and ligaments are ripped and muscles have no lean meat on them. Men and women are weaker in the areas that count and yet are larger in the areas that are unhealthy to be large in, like the waist. All this puts harmful stress on the heart and circulation system and the body can't heal itself each day as it needs to."

"After a long hard day at work," Grandma continued, "I would fall into bed with my essential oil of lavender mixed delicately with a carrier oil for soothing my skin and restoring the shine and moisture within. Upon waking, my skin would be repaired from the sun damage feeling clean and looking shiny. Of course, I always added a bit of vitamin E for extra softness. The lovely aroma of the lavender helped me to fall asleep each night by relaxing my body and calming my mind. It also helped to relieve stress I was feeling and all the while, it was acting as a tonic, cleansing me on the inside.

Essential Oils are the healing fragrances in life that don't attack organs negatively, but rather they heal by stimulating and cleansing organs so they can give us very healthy bodies. Take the liver for example, it's a filter for the blood stream and when this filter is clean, it removes impurities from our bodies that we've ingested and inhaled throughout the day. When this filter is plugged, the body will shut down, or it just won't start up, similarly to your car when the fuel filter is plugged and no gasoline gets to the engine. The engine won't run. The body is the same way. Plug up the blood stream and the body won't function.

And Emma, the greatest part about these essential oils is the price point. They are so inexpensive when compared to perfumes. The oil used in mixing them is regular eating oils that have healing properties of their own. When I want to create household cleaning products, I use a combination of clean water, rubbing alcohol to kill germs and essential oils that are great for disinfectants, antiseptics, cleansers, eliminating viruses, funguses, bacteria and parasites. They generally smell great giving me strength, and energy lifting my spirits all the while I'm cleaning the house. I can't for the life of me understand why anyone would want to use chemicals that are harmful to the body when these oils and products clean, protect and in most cases do an even better job than any product I've ever bought. And the cost is comparable and can be even more cost effective. Plus, I know what's in my cleaner. Imagine you just cleaned your bathroom and it smells fresh like wintergreen or floral like rose geranium, or forest smelling, like Scotch pine. Now imagine you wash your hands and they smell spicy like cinnamon and clove or fresh and lively like pink grapefruit. Imagine your body floating in a field of fresh grapefruits and your mouth waters for its juicy, sweet taste."

And so I envisioned what she described and I found myself pleasantly floating in a field filled with grapefruit trees while I picked the juicy ones and then drifted into the white fluffy clouds and baby blue sky.

On other occasions, Grandma was blunt and didn't mind talking about what happened to her body, like the time she told me about what happens during menopause, which was unheard of to talk about openly in her day. I guess I was fortunate to have my grandmother because from her, I learned not to be shy about my sexuality.

In her sexual years, Grandma said almond oil was more than a skin moisturizer and massage oil, it was also a woman's great friend in bed. It provided a thick barrier for lubricating which was to be very important to women in their menopause years as it gave a helpful moisturizing effect for the entire area. Men would benefit from it too as it has vitamins D and E which their manliness could use.

"Of course, Emma, eating foods rich in estrogen and progesterone will be helpful to you in your aging years. Too little estrogen causes the hair to grow on your upper lip and chin, which, you can tweeze out if you desire to do so," she said.

I often felt silly, rather embarrassed really, when Grandma said things like that to me and I didn't know if they were true or not. But, I was to find out, she was right.

Home Fragrant Spray:

Small spray bottle 50-100 ml

1 tbsp rubbing alcohol

½ tsp essential oil of your choice.......adjust for strength according to preference, 10-40 drops

Top up with clean water

Body Massage Oil

Grape seed oil, anti wrinkling, toning

olive oil, moisturizing

almond oil, moisturizing, Vitamins D and E

Use any of the above oils, or a mixture of all three, combine with

Vitamin E oil 1/8 -1/4 tsp and

Your favourite essential oil such as Ylang-ylang, Peppermint and Rosemary, Clove, Lemongrass, Lavender, Grapefruit, and Orange

TIP:

Light tasting olive oil mixes best with heavier essential oils such as clove and eucalyptus avoiding the pungent odour of the olives.

26

ECOLOGICAL FOOTPRINT

"Earth provides enough to satisfy every man's needs, but not every man's greed."
-- Gandhi

Examining my lip gloss tube from a well known and reputable company, I started thinking of how I could reuse this slender dispenser that had a nice plastic body with built in interior gears and a helical plunger designed to push the lip gloss up and out the small opening at the tip where a rubber glider was housed, allowing the gloss to be applied smoothly over my lips. It was a luxurious and decadent way of getting smooth lips.

The cap contained a small plastic stem that neatly fit over the rubber applicator preventing the small opening from being plugged with the gloss during the times it was not being used. "Wow," I said to myself out loud. "This is a well thought out dispensing system that contains moving parts and it's made to be disposable and not reusable." Thinking about this, I remembered that it was the dispenser that captured my attention in the first place and as a consumer I loved carrying it around with me. It didn't leak, it looked pretty and the applicator was easy to use and luxurious. So yes, I would love to refill it with my own lip protector that Grandma so cleverly taught me to make but I can't because this unit was made for one time use and not refillable by the consumer. I'm sure the company had it's reasons for making it this way, but as my grandmother would say, "if its not reusable, then think about whether or not you really have to have it before you buy it." Ah yes, it was a great lip gloss, but this girl is going to skip on the second new purchase and make her own this time, instead, applying it with a refillable dispenser.

Grandma routinely splashed cold water on her face throughout the day to keep it hydrated and then rubbed a small amount of almond or grape seed oil on her cheeks and mouth area to seal in the moisture. Grandma had smooth, shiny skin and she always looked years younger than her age. Combined with the goodness of making her own products, Grandma didn't have much waste in her garbage and so she thought of herself as environmentally friendly even before the termed was coined as such. I loved telling her that and she guffawed at me saying, "make your own skin products, eat plenty of fruits and vegetables, compost the waste and exercise often and you will be fit and energetic and the environment will love you for it."

To her it was that simple and when I thought about her ecological footprint in the world, I thought she was likely one of the few people who actually grew and replaced more than she took out. Along with vegetable and herb gardens, she planted various trees in her land, including some evergreens for Christmas trees ensuring she planted more each year than she sold. Even her house is no longer standing as a building but is now a field lush with wild animals and thick greenery.

Grandma heated her house only to a comfortable setting knowing she could put on sweaters and warm clothing when required.

"Being cooler is better for the body," she reminded me. "Coupled with exercise, the blood will flow warming your body, keeping you healthy. It's never good to sit around too long because it reduces the flow of blood and circulation in the body. There're activities to engage in and by being busy, your body will stay fit and warm and you won't have to heat your house so much in the winter, either."

Maybe this was just her way of keeping the heating bills low, of accepting the ways of her life on a budget, and of getting work done, but whatever it was about, it is how she lived and never was I cold in Grandma's house, not with all those warm sweaters she knitted and all that fresh baking and cooking going on, heating up the kitchen.

Making lip gloss and lip moisturizer with Grandma was fun and simple. We mixed together,

Lip Gloss

1 tsp of honey

1 tbsp of food grade oil of choice as follows:

Almond Oil to heal dry, cracked lips

Grape Seed Oil to tone fine lines around lips

1/8 tsp or 1 capsule (squeezed) of Vitamin E oil

TIP:

For red or pink lips, we included a tiny dab of Amaranth that Grandma grew in her garden. It's also found in some health food stores.

27

PATIENCE AND IMPATIENS

"If I had a flower for every time I thought of you...I could walk through my garden forever." -- Alfred Tennyson

Among tulips, hydrangeas, daffodils and impatiens, my favourite spring time flowers are impatiens. Their flowers are bright and cheerful and can light up any dark and shady part of the yard. I find growing impatiens to be quite easy. If the seedlings are given the right conditions, they will sprout and grow quickly.

Grandma told me that impatiens flowers remind us all to be patient, calm and tolerant with people and processes. She also told me we should try to understand the people, take the time to listen, and check out facts before making our decisions. She equated impatiens with the discovery of the Bach Rescue Remedy whereby the belief is that by selecting the oral tinctures according to specific feelings, the body could be allowed to heal naturally. This remedy, I'm told by Grandma while doing gardening with her one cool spring day, was invented in the 1930's by a Dr Edward Bach. She explained to me that the idea behind using flowers and plants to balance emotions and moods was one so popular and powerful that it has its own branch of science. Homeopathy, aromatherapy and naturopathy are just a few of the branches of health care that subscribe to the use of plants and flowers helping people with their everyday checks and balances and mood swings. Grandma told me she had read all about impatiens having a calming effect on a person and that was just one of the positive aspects of eating them and of using them in homeopathy. Comfort, rational thought, courage and focus were some others Grandma mentioned, but it was the calming aspect she focused on because it was thought that the impatiens used were the reason homeopathic tinctures could provide this calming effect.

"Mental and emotional agitation may be soothed and you may feel more patient and less restless, Dear." It sounded like a line from a commercial, I thought.

"Have you ever tried it, Grandma?"

"No, but I have eaten the flowers of the impatiens plants and while they didn't offer much in the way of flavour, they did add a colourful display to the food on the plate and the meal did look much more eloquent." Grandma continued, as she bent over using the mini trowel in her right hand to dig into the dirt with while her left hand pulled up the loosened weed, roots and all, so that it was gone from the side garden where her beautiful red impatiens bloomed.

"Did you feel different after you ate it?"

Giving this some thought, Grandma stood up to straighten her spine and stretch her hip muscles by slightly bending side to side and back and forth. She put her left hand on her hip and with her right hand still holding the trowel, she reached up with her thumb to clear the hair from her forehead and away from her eyes, leaving behind a mark of mud between her eyebrows. I chuckled when I saw this. With eyes looking at me and eyebrows narrowed in, she asked, "and just what do you find to be so funny, little missy?"

"It's you, Grandma; you have mud on your face."

"Ah, the irony in that," replied my grandmother.

"Don't tell me mud in your face is healthy too?"

"Well, actually it can be, but I'll leave that for the spa. Today, I'll tell you about another meaning of the phrase, mud in my face," Grandma began her story.

"It was the day of the dinner where I ate the impatiens. I was just eighteen and the year was 1937. The world was such an exciting place then, but it was scary too with the tides of change coming and not all for the good either. It was the year when the US Army Air Corps physiological research laboratory was completed in Ohio, and when the soap opera "Guiding Light" premièred on radio becoming one of my favourite pass times and when US Steel raised their workers' wages to $5 a day which later had impact on your grandfather's employment. It was when Margaret Mitchell won the Pulitzer Prize for 'Gone with the Wind' which I know is your favourite movie, Emma."

"You remember so much, Grandma," I exclaimed in awe of her perfect memory. Something I wish I had inherited from her, but unfortunately wasn't very good at.

"Thank you, Dear. But I only remember all this because it had an impact on my life and it brought meaning to so much of what went on in the future. Events have a way of marking turning points in people's lives and in helping to shape what the world will become for us."

"And back to the events of the time," Grandma went on. "As I was saying, George VI was crowned King of England and the German battleships bombed Spain. And last but not least, 1937 was when the world's largest flower bloomed in New York Botanical Gardens. It was a twelve foot calla lily and it was all the rage. No one had ever heard of or seen a 12 foot calla lily before then but it was such an event, our whole town celebrated it even though it grew far from here. We celebrated it because we all felt like we were a part of its success with flowers and gardens being such a large part of our own lives."

"It was also the year I was invited to a dinner party by my mother's best friend who frequently entertained military officers while they were away from home. Madame I called her, but I was never allowed to add a name to the title. It was never explained to me why she didn't have a name and I didn't dare ask. I remember seeing my father carrying a shoe box once a month to the local police station where he left the shoe box. From my bedroom window, I saw him leaving Madame's large, mysterious house, walk down the street in his usual handsome manner, carrying the shoe box and looking so official and serious. He had such a straight walking posture and he appeared to be proud, never missing a month. Later in life, I did ask about the shoe box and was told it contained money. Money for what though, I never found out. I always assumed it was for all the great work the police did in our community and I knew Madame wasn't a great cook so she couldn't offer meals to the officers like the other women in the town could, and so I figured with Madame being rich and all, this was how she cared for them. No one ever tried to change my thinking.

So on the night of this one dinner party, I entered the foyer of the grand old house and saw rich thick fabric sewn into elaborate curtains contrasting dark hard wood flooring made from solid maple. I could tell the different kinds of wood that the furniture and floorings were made from because I loved trees. I could appreciate all the intricate details and the wear on the varnishes of the furniture and floors and I understood how long a tree had to live and grow to supply enough of its wood for these purposes. To me, the tree was still alive and breathing and I was grateful for the opportunity to touch and feel it under my feet and hands.

But I digress. Upon entering the foyer, I also saw a tall handsome man who appeared to be distant, uncomfortable and not easy to be around. His clothing didn't reveal much about him and it was hard to know what his character was like just by sizing him up. With a clenched fist, he discreetly handed Madame something wearing a happy smile while nodding loosely and bowing slightly in her direction before exiting.

Seeing me standing there, Madame scurried over to where I stood, and while helping me to take my shawl from my shoulders, exclaimed loudly with her vibrant voice the way that only Madame could have."

"Bella! How delightful you decided to come. You are such a splendid looking creature what with your fine bones and sturdy legs and arms. Surely, you do spend too much of your time in the sun and gardens, though. You ought not to do that to your skin, you know; it will make it dreadfully difficult to find you a suitable husband should you look old before your time. We must find you a man who will spoil you by buying nice clothes and a grand house, like this one, for you to live in. And he will hire someone to work in your gardens for you."

"Ah, Madame, you know I don't care for that sort of thing," Grandma replied smartly. "And you know I don't fuss or worry about my skin as I have botanicals and oils to freshen it every day, making it just like it was when I was a baby, sometimes better."

"You put too much faith into that stuff, my young lass. One day you will be old and wrinkly and will wish you had heeded Madame's advice."

"Perhaps, but not at this time. To what do I owe the pleasure of your company by way of this dinner invitation? It was a surprise to me receiving your invitation with such short notice, although you know I am always delighted to be a guest at one of your parties."

"Tonight, my love, I will introduce you to the man of your dreams and perhaps to the future father of your children."

"Oh, Madame, why do you trouble yourself so?" Grandma asked. "You know I want to do my studies and become the greatest nurse and then homeopath in the country. I want to heal people, Madame, and make them well using nature's gifts. I once read a quote from the bible that explained how God put all kinds of things on this earth to keep us healthy and how we have everything here we'll ever need. Madame, I feel the power of healing in my very spirit and in everything I do all day long. The plants can heal us. They can make us all well and remove anything harmful from our bodies. They are so beautiful, Madame, and I want to share all that with the world. But first, I have to learn about it all and then get a license to practice so people will believe me. Madame, if you can find a husband for me that will allow me to do all that as his wife, then I'll be elated. Do you think this man here tonight would be supportive enough to allow me my indulgences as his wife?"

"Nonsense, Belle. Why on earth would you want that from a man?"

"Because," Rosa Belle answered, "it is my calling."

Not knowing what to do with that or how to respond, Madame ushered everyone into her dining room beginning the night's festivities. Seating Belle next to the handsome man, Madame had hoped she had found Belle her perfect mate.

But as it was, this man was not to be the one for the magnificent Rosa Belle as he could not tolerate her ambition and thirst for a different kind of world. Madame became very upset with her for not trying harder to develop a lasting relationship with him, and upon Belle's departure that evening, she wished Belle a pleasant life, but under her breathe, Madame uttered, "May you, Belle, be cursed with a lazy and drunken husband."

It was a mere three months later that Grandma and Grandpa married, in the year 1937.

28

PEDICURES

"Take care of your body. It's the only place you have to live."
-- Jim Rohn

Spa days with Grandma were some of the best days ever. She made her own treatment products from ingredients she had in her pantry and then gave them extra boost and 'healing' properties by adding essential oils. The aroma from the essential oils gave a mood boost and set the atmosphere for the day. On warm days that needed cooling, Scotch pine or peppermint oils were added to give a refreshing, cooling feeling. For days that circulation needed boosting, warm oils such as clove and cinnamon were used, and for days when relaxation and stress relief was sought after, lavender oil was favoured. I loved lemon grass for the energizing and refreshing effects it had on my spirit. I could never decide which oil was my absolute favourite because each one had a slightly different effect for me and I decided which one to use based on my feeling that day. I gently sniffed the small brown bottle the oil came in and the one that pleased my senses the most is the one I chose. For this reason, I never mixed my oils ahead of time, but always just at the moment I was about to use it.

Eucalyptus was for days when my breathing wasn't quite right or for when I had a cold. To this day, I mix eucalyptus essential oil in my body oil on a regular basis. It's the greatest smell when used in the sauna and steam room because of its refreshing and clean scent. It helps me to breathe by opening my air ways and bronchial tubes and because I'm breathing deeper and easier, my muscle pain is relieved due to the increased oxygen circulating to them.

Grandma said essential oils have healing properties in them.

"They enter the body through your senses, Emma, and they help the body to reawaken itself." And so it was that Grandma kept a healthy supply of essential oils to mix in with all her personal moisturizing and cleaning products as well as in her household cleaning products.

"Fragrant oils are synthetic," she commented to me often, "and have a way of attacking the body and its organs, whereas essential oils are healing oils that the body responds to helping the body to reach equilibrium."

For perfume, bergamot and rose geranium essential oils were her favourite right through her entire life. Pedicures to Grandma meant sandpaper, graters, water, almond oil, tea tree essential oil and hot summer days down by the creek. Sitting at the edge of the stream that ran through her back yard, Grandma spent some hot summer days decadently spoiling her feet, all the while day dreaming of having acres and acres of elegant gardens, listening to dinner jazz music while entertaining friends and family and of being a famous Homeopath. But for Grandma, these were just fantasies. She was content enough with her life and had no desire to actually change it once it's course had been set.

Sitting on a large rock deep in the woods of her backyard, Grandma used her old and broken down handheld grater to give herself a pedicure. She used the four sides of the grater to remove calluses from her feet and then smoothed them to a fine finish with a light grade of sand paper. Grandma never had enough money to get a professional pedicure done, but she sure did have beautiful feet. Grandma always took care of herself as best as she could by using the oddest things around the house that were available to her.

The grater served as the tool to remove the harden dried skin and the nail filer served as the tool to fine tune and soften the area of the feet that were most prone to calluses. Grandpa made an emery board filer for her to do her feet with by shellacking 2 grades of sandpaper to a wooden handle so Grandma could file the bottoms of her feet coarsely and finely. By shellacking it, the tool became waterproof so Grandma could use it while soaking her feet, making the harden skin softer and easier to scrape away. Tea Tree essential oil was added by the drop to sweet almond oil and rubbed on her feet as a moisturizer and skin protector.

"The tea tree oil provides antibacterial properties that will help to keep fungus away from feet and toe nails,' she explained to me, while trying to inspire me to do the same with my feet. It has a pleasant smell and can be mixed with other essential oils such as clove, cinnamon, sage, geranium, lavender, and rosemary. All of which will help with the circulation and healing of the foot too."

For quick hydration of her skin, she cut stems from her Aloe Vera plant, sliced open the leaf and rubbed the gel flesh over her face, neck, hands, arms, legs and feet. By doing this, her skin was quickly healed of the small cuts, scratches and sun burns she received from being in her gardens.

I envied Grandma her ability to live the exquisite life in her dreams while being one of the poorest people, financially, I knew. Grandma never had enough money, but she had stuff. Somehow the stuff appeared from others and what seemed like out of nowhere. Grandma didn't have cash or savings, neither on her nor in her bank account and she certainly never went to the spa for facials or manicures and pedicures. The food she ate was from the ground she lived on. By the work of her own hands, Grandma raised livestock, grew food in gardens and harvested the seeds, sharing them with her neighbours so all the seeds would be fresh and healthy. She started her seeds in water and then planted them to produce delicious and hearty vegetables all summer long. No one in the community had nicer or healthier gardens than Grandma. The neighbours from miles around would say, 'Now just look at her gardens grow! And never a weed among them. How does she do it?'

She worked hard at it, that's how. She got muddy, calloused, sweaty and tired and so the days she spent down by the creek were called her spa days where she relaxed her mind and body, pampered her feet with pedicures, smoothened her fine lines and skin with homemade facials and gave herself mud baths using the peat from the marsh. This was when Grandma put peat moss mud on her face and called it healthy. She said it pulled toxins out from within her skin and in doing so, it left her body fresh and rejuvenated. She loved her mud body treatments.

After her spa treatments, Grandma coated her skin in almond oil and allowed it to soak in to moisturize and soothe her all over. Any excess was wiped off with a dry towel. Her complexion was bright and her skin was soft as silk, not what I would have expected from someone who was such a hard physical worker out in the hot sun in the summer and the cold weather in the winter.

In the early days of Grandma's life when she didn't have a hot water tank in her house, she took her winter baths indoors in a large soaker metal tub. Hot water was heated on top of the wood stove and then poured into the tub, mixing it with cold water from the tap. I was happy when Grandma had a hot water heater installed in her house so she was able to have warm baths all year round, and not just when the wood stove was lit. In her baths,

Grandma insisted on adding baking soda.

"Grandma, look!" little Emma exclaimed, "The bath water is sizzling."

"Those are carbon dioxide bubbles being released in the water from the baking soda, and it looks like its sizzling. The bubbles are forming and then breaking, stirring up the water," Grandma explained.

"Why do you put baking soda in the bath anyway?" Emma inquired.

"Soda is added, Emma, because it drains the lymphatic system of toxins and disease. Most people think only Epsom salts remove toxins, but baking soda does too. And what's the lymphatic system, you're going to ask next? It's the part of the body that helps to fight infections and disease and so it must be cleaned regularly and baking soda will do just that. Putting it in the bath soothes the skin, drains the lymphatic system and helps to keep us healthy," she patiently explained.

Grandma's bath was even more interesting to me when I saw her putting oatmeal into one of her old nylons which she said she used as her 'puff' in the bath. The oatmeal turned into a gooey substance once it was wetted but when Grandma rubbed her body with it, her skin became soft and clean and the oatmeal dissolved in the bath water.

And so the day I became infected with poison ivy from a field nearby, Grandma soaked me in a bath with baking soda and oatmeal and my skin rash was instantly soothed. But to cure the poison ivy, Grandma used a different, more natural method that I don't talk about, but I still will use it today if the need arises, because it works too.

Grandma was very encouraging about using aromatherapy every day, but colour therapy was more subtle. Everyone knew that colours affected mood and we all had our favourite colour, but Grandma knew how to use colour in her bath to set her mood. She put several drops of food colouring in her bath water along with her baking soda, bath salts, and essential oils to make the whole mood and environment conducive to luxury and peace.

Sometimes she made her water blue for peace, tranquility and calmness and sometimes she made it green for liveliness, energy, balance, harmony and love. And when she had her relaxing baths with lavender, she made the water purple by mixing red and blue together. She taught me to use a few drops of food colouring in my bath water to help set a mood I was trying to create. I found it was a bit difficult to wash the colouring off the bath tub and so I stopped doing this, but Grandma had no problems with it because she owned the old porcelain tubs that didn't stain like the newer plastic tubs that I have today. But I do use food colouring in my foot soak baths and in my porcelain sink when I'm having a 'spa day' at home, just not in my plastic tub.

Sesame Oil Skin Wash

Rub pure (unrefined) sesame oil on skin including face and allow oil to soak in for a few minutes removing black heads and oils from within the skin.
Rinse with warm water, using a facecloth to remove excess oil.
TIP: This is particularly soothing to skin while sitting in a bath or a steam room.

Almond Oil moisturizer

Rub pure sweet almond oil over body including face and eye area and allow to soak in, removing excessive oil by further rubbing or with a dry damp cloth.
TIP: Almond Oil is very moisturizing and can be applied to the hair at night time making it soft and shiny.

Face Wash that Brightens Skin

1 part castile soap

1 part freshly squeezed lemon juice or bottled lemon juice

Several Drops of essential oils lemon and lemon grass (grapefruit is also favourable)

Mix together in a squeeze or pump bottle. Will last several weeks.

TIP: Follow up with almond or grape seed oil for moisturizing and toning properties.

Moisturizing Hand Wash For softer hands, especially in the winter time

1 cup of favourite unscented hand cream

20-40 drops of essential oils of your preference

4 tbsp almond oil

Combine ingredients together, stir and then transfer to a pump or plastic squeeze bottle.

Liquid Foundation

Mica, gold and beige

Cream base

Mix equal parts of both micas and 6 parts cream and blend together.

(Cheat: add a tiny bit of dark foundation for starter colour and base)

Powder foundation (mineral)

Mica, gold and beige

Cornstarch

Mix one part cornstarch with 2 parts mica.

Antiperspirant

Mix together equal parts Vodka or 99% grade Rubbing Alcohol, Liquid Witch Hazel, and Distilled/Filtered Water or Liquid Aloe for dry skin (aloe is soothing for skin).

Add 20-40 drops Essential Oil of your choice (smell oil before adding to find your scent).

Suggestions are: Rosewood, Elemi, Tea Tree, Rosemary, Sage, Lavender, Ylang-Ylang, Clove, Peppermint (for cooling), Bergamot, Grapefruit, Lemon, Lemongrass, Orange, Scotch Pine, Rose Geranium.

Combine together in a spray bottle and apply after washing.

TIPS:

Solution too dry on your skin? Add a couple of drops of vitamin E liquid to mixture.

Protection not effective enough? Remove water and aloe.

Some essential oils blend together better than others, so start with only a single and gradually add others as you become familiar with your preferences.

Elemi essential oil is a good anti microbial and when mixed with Tea Tree, Scotch Pine, Rosewood and Rosemary makes for an effective man's antiperspirant.

Curly Waves Hair Spray (need to have wavy hair for this to work)

1 cup water (alternate: aloe juice for hydration),

1 orange

2 tbsp 99% rubbing alcohol

10 drops orange essential oil

Cut orange into quarters and place in a pot with water (or aloe juice).

Boil on med heat (covered) for 30 mins but do not allow the liquid to boil dry.

Once reduced, allow mixture to cool and then strain into a spray bottle.

Add rubbing alcohol and essential oil.

Will keep in frig for several months.

Variation:

Use a lemon or grapefruit instead of the orange and then use the essential oil to match (lemon with lemon and grapefruit with grapefruit).

TIP: For a stronger hold, boil mixture longer producing a stickier solution then add an additional tablespoon of rubbing alcohol if required allowing it to spray easily.

The Ultimate Bath Soak

½ cup baking soda

½ cup Epsom salts

20-30 drops of your favourite essential Oil, including eucalyptus, peppermint, orange, rose, lavender.

Tip: Smell the essential oil before pouring into bath water to determine what you are in the mood for that day. The most pleasant smelling oil is the one you should pick.

Note: more than one essential oil can be used at the same time to blend aromatic effects.

Variation:

Adding 1 cup of uncooked rolled oats to bath water will help to soften skin. The oats will dissolve in the water.

Similarly, adding 1 cup of whole milk to the bath water will also soften skin.

29

A MOTHER'S SCORN

"Oh my son's my son till he gets a wife, but my daughter's my daughter all her life." -- Dinah Mulock Craik

The hurt that comes from a mother's scorn can be the most debilitating hurt of all. Grandma never could explain to me why the women in her family couldn't get along. All through the generations, she told me, "some women in my family have been angry at each other for decades. As much as we've been here for each other, the jabs, barbs and general dislikes for each other have been the most noticeable trait in our family; that and the fact that we've never been able to keep a dime in our pockets."

Remembering the time I sat in a restaurant with my mother and her cousin, Linda, who was my great aunt Abby's daughter, I felt the tension in the air. The weather was hot and muggy but the breeze from the lake was cooling and refreshing. Looking for a seat on the patio overlooking the boats moored to the docks, we saw the boat owners socializing with each other, noticing that many of them had set up ten foot by ten foot canopy tents to sit under, extending the use of the docking area. BBQ's and small bar refrigerators sat among the patio tables and lounge chairs where the boaters drank their beverages and soaked up the sunshine. The water in the docking area was a muddy brown so no one was swimming, but not far away was the opening to the lake where the boaters cruised to their destinations on the captivating blue water. The land across the Great Lake could just barely be seen by the naked eye, the lake was so large.

Finding a table in the shade of the trees growing within the restaurant's deck, the three of us sat facing the water thinking about our drink orders.

"Have you seen my new ring?" my mother asked her cousin.

"No, let me see it," Linda replied showing interest.

Reaching over the table, my mother proudly displayed her new ring to her cousin Linda, who marveled over how beautiful it was with its many colours and intertwined patterns. "I bought this last week when I was at my son's house, visiting," Mom explained. "We went shopping and when I saw it, I thought how I just had to buy it. It's just like the ones I see in the Caribbean."

"Emerald, have you seen it?" she asked leaning in my direction, extending her hand into my face.

"Yes, I saw it and it's very nice." I carefully replied.

Looking over my shoulder, I noticed a new purse sitting on the ground. "Is that a new purse, too?" I asked.

"Yes, I'm being laughed at now because I always comment on how large Linda's purse is compared to my small ones. I've often told her that she doesn't need a big purse to carry all that stuff around in and that my small one is better, but now, here I sit with a large purse and I really like it. I can fill it up with so many useful things."

"But Mom, you always carried a large purse when I was growing up. It's just been in the last fifteen years that you started carrying a waist sack or small shoulder bag. You started that when you began travelling because you said you could keep your coins and passport close to you carrying it around on your body without having to worry about losing a bag or being pickpocketed," I went on.

Looking at me with her brown eyes, Mom calmly changed the subject and gave her order to the waitress who had just appeared.

"Will this all be on one bill, or separate bills?" the waitress asked.

"Two bills, actually," my mother spoke out. "I'll be paying for yours, Linda, and Emerald, I'll pay for yours when I'm rich."

"That'll never happen," I replied tartly, knowing my mother all too well. If there was money in her pocket, she'd gamble it away or spend it on something she didn't need or travel abroad with it. Disappearing for much of my childhood, she travelled the world for work and during those working trips, she played the slots and card games, partied her way through life, and took numerous lovers in affairs, showing to me that she would never be a rich woman. And yet, rich she was with children, a husband and a home, but she didn't know it. My mother complained about everything and threw it all away. It's the one consistent thing I remember about her. And yet, every day of the week, my mother had enough food on her plate to keep her overweight knowing she could eat chicken or any other meat everyday if she wanted. She had designer clothes filling her closets beyond their capacity, her house had been filled with art and paintings and beautiful furniture, her cupboards were stocked with packaged foods, her small lap dog had both wet and dry foods and snacks, her fish aquarium was filled with tropical fish, her car was always filled with gas and was fully paid for, she lived in one of the richest countries in the world, had healthy children, went on vacations, shopped everyday of the week, and yet she always claimed she didn't have enough. She confused not being rich with not having enough money for everything in the world she wanted and that was something that always bothered me. When Mom looked at me, she looked angry as though somehow this was my fault. It's with this anger that I often wondered why I bothered to have a relationship with my mother at all but then I remembered my grandmother's words about the women in my family never getting along and never being able to keep a dime in their pockets. I will have to be sure to change that pattern when I have my own family, I told myself as I returned to my home after lunch to sit on my front porch and admire my own gardens, just as my grandmother admired hers.

"It's a good thing we're great at living off the land, you and I," Grandma's words came to me. "Keep your gardens free from weeds and you'll eat like a queen all year round. We're among the richest people in the world living where we do with all this warmth, sunshine, rain and fertile soil. We can grow a variety of crops that are nutritious and plentiful like, broccoli, corn, radishes, potatoes, beets, carrots, peas, beans, asparagus, tomatoes squash, zucchini, lettuce, garlic, onions, leeks, tomatoes, grapes, cherries, apples, peaches, strawberries, grapes and so much more too. We're incredibly blessed to have the right conditions to grow all this food right here in our own backyards. It was such a disappointment to me that I could never convince your mother to embrace it all. It's a good thing for me that I have you, Emerald, dear."

When Grandma talked about our own backyards, she was talking about the southern reaches in the province of Ontario. Grandma loved living here and talked quite readily about it. Lakes in the summer, green fields with gardens and farm animals in the spring, summer and fall, and delightful snow in the winter. "The snow,: she reminded me, "is what freshens up our dull gray winters and turns everything a pristine white."

In the winter, the trees and animals hibernated, the soil froze and the whole area became a playground for all those who embraced it. Even chores in the winter could be enjoyed when the morning sun shone upon the snow covered ground, glistening and sparkling, creating what I liked to call a winter wonderland of magical fairy dust. Sometimes when the sun hit the snow dust falling from the branches of a nearby tree, it created a sparkling golden sheen that glistened and spread magic to those who saw it, and when I saw it, I would think to myself, I'm a princess in the snow, and I'd say a prayer wishing for my heart's deepest desires to be fulfilled. I deeply breathed in the fresh crisp air and knew it was great to be alive and living in this beautiful land.

My grandmother was rich and so then, was I.

30

TODAY THE SKY IS GRAY AND THE AIR IS COLD

"Nothing can dim the light which shines from within." -- Maya Angelou

Today the sky was gray and the air cold. No warmth, no beaches, no sunshine. I tried to lift my spirits, so I left work early to go to the department store to buy a hair dye that would brighten my mood. Even my roots were gray.

I bought some pepperoni sticks, hair dye and rubbing alcohol that I'd use as a bathroom disinfectant by mixing it in a spray bottle with water and my favourite essential oil. Today it will be something floral to remind me of spring even though I know spring is many months away.

Once back home, I found myself sitting in my living room with my laptop open doing my work assignment in between sipping tea and glimpsing the television, watching a movie about friends who were having a relationship together just for the fun of it. I ate a bag of potato chips, two sticks of pepperoni and then drank a can of beer. Sex; there's that word again. It has no meaning to me, only that it's something other people have.

I checked the mail but nothing good was in it, only bills. Bills that I couldn't really afford to pay so I paid them from my line of credit.

My hair was ready to wash now so I made my way to the shower to wash out the dye. My scalp was itchy but I followed up with the conditioner they gave me in the box and rinsed it all out. Upstairs I dried my hair with the blower while the flat iron heated up. My scalp was still itchy. Opening the bag the cosmetic lady gave me at the store filled with little 'treats' as she called them, I looked at the hydrating face serum that came in a cute bronze capsule that required me only to snip the tip off and apply to my cleanly washed face. Looking in the mirror, I saw no changes to my dry skin so I followed up with my own products. Grandma would have been so disappointed in me today if she found out I used a chemical based dye instead of my usual vegetable dye that had no peroxide in it. The peroxide is probably what was making my scalp itchy, but then again, it may have been from the other chemicals in it too. Oh, I should never venture from my natural dye that feels so refreshing and smooth. But because of my down mood today, I thought I'd go for more shine having seen a commercial on television the night before. What a mistake.

Looking at my face again in the mirror, I saw my skin still needed more hydrating, probably as a result of the bad food and drink I was consuming, so just as my grandmother showed me, I splashed fresh cool water on my skin and then lightly patted it to damp dry with a clean cloth. I then reached into my medicine cabinet and pulled out the avocado and almond oil mixed with my favourite edible grape seed oil. Wanting some additional softness, I added a touch of honey to my oil. Fragrance, I need a pick me up fragrance. Reaching back into the medicine cabin, I searched for the essential oil that made me feel alive. Today it's lemon. Pouring some concentrated lemon essential oil onto the palm of my hand, I mixed it into the oil and then I lightly spread it across my face, throat, and chest. Breathing deeply, I felt the energizing effects of the oil already, and a giant smile crossed my face as

I began to relax, looking and feeling better.

Back downstairs again, I continued watching my movie, feeling good and smelling fresh from the lemon....but my scalp, it was still itchy. Note to self; always use your vegetable dye. If this itchiness gets too bad, I'll put some almond oil on my scalp to sooth and moisturize it, just like Grandma showed me. And tomorrow, I will eat healthier.

While watching the movie, I couldn't help but to think of my mother, her image constantly running through my mind. Every now and then, I get into these dark moods as I ponder the relationship I have with her. Our relationship always seemed strained, and always had been, yet I didn't know why exactly. I'm careful not to follow in her footsteps because I don't want the choices she made in her life to be for my own life. I have dreams and visions of my own, and yet, I do respect that my parents had visions for their life, but they also had visions for my life too, visions that don't align with what I want. My mom and I don't share the same ideas of how I should live and as such, it seemed she didn't take an interest in me from the onset. It felt like she didn't try to understand me as a person and this eventually led to our arguing because I resisted her ideas, wishing she could be a greater leader for me or a better guiding influence. I worried about her judgement and was actually scared to be like her. But when God closes a door, he opens a window. He gave me Grandma and He gave me some shared moments with my mother, such as when we played baseball or those times when Mom and I made chocolate pudding together.

Chocolate pudding was a favourite of mine and I will always associate it with my mom. When we made it, the pudding turned out creamy, smooth and chocolaty and it gave us the opportunity to have two days together. The pudding was cooked and left to chill in the afternoon of the first day, and then whipped, chilled again and eaten the next day, and so we had two whole days together and at the end of it, we had the pure pleasure of eating chocolate!

Over the years, Mom and I did become closer as we learned to understand each other better. She began to be thoughtful, slowly at first, but then it became more natural, and she showed consideration, learning to appreciate that I too have dreams and desires. In return, I began having more patience with her, tolerating her lifestyle and forgiving her for being absent for much of my childhood. This forgiveness allowed us to have a peaceful relationship together into our aging years and my mother became a very good grandmother to my own children, giving to them what she had denied me. Could it be that through the blessings of a grandmother, God is able to provide the healing pathway between mother and daughter? I won't know the full answer to that question, but in my own life, that sure rang true.

Chocolate Pudding (similar to Vanilla Pudding, chapter 8)

Ingredients

2 ½ cups whole milk or 2%
½ cup sugar
9 tbsp cocoa powder or 3 squares of unsweetened chocolate
¼ tsp salt
½ cup good quality cornstarch
2 tbsp pure vanilla extract

Instructions

1. In a medium sized pot on the stove, combine milk, sugar, cocoa powder, salt and cornstarch. Whisk together over medium heat.
2. When milk mixture begins to warm, use a wooden spoon to constantly stir and reduce heat to low. Allow mixture to heat and thicken while

stirring constantly. This takes about 20 minutes.

3. Once thickened, remove from heat and add vanilla, stirring in thoroughly.

4. Pour pudding into mixing bowl and allow to cool for an hour before placing in refrigerator overnight to set. Plastic wrap can used to cover mixing bowl if desired.

5. Next day, whip pudding in the mixing bowl using high speed hand held mixer, until smooth and creamy, but still thick.

6. Place pudding back in refrigerator for an hour to continue chilling. Pudding will then be ready to eat.

31

PRAYER

"The function of prayer is not to influence God, but rather to change the nature of the one who prays." -- Soren Kierkegaard

Even though I knew I had so much, similar to how my mother had been, I wanted more. I wanted the freedom and at the same time, the responsibility that came with more, and so I knew I had to pray to change. Being beautiful on the inside, happy, full of energy and rich meant a lot to me. I thought it meant I would have the power to influence decisions, the ability to do God's Will and the chance of a life time to experience the world with all the goodness it has to offer. There're so many great opportunities out there and so many beautiful things to see and experience such as traveling, scenery, animals and birds. Birds. Why, just last week, a beautiful robin landed on the grass of the golf course where I was playing nine holes. It had fallen to its side with an injured wing. Looking around, I saw many robins flying in circles, nesting for the evening. But this one beautiful robin missed the landing on the tree branch and in doing so, injured its wing. Falling to the ground, this robin felt its vulnerability, and I could tell this because it looked me straight in the eye while it lay on its side with its injured wing upward, resting. Staring at me, its soul looked into mine, trusting me not to harm it in its paralyzed state. At least the birds hadn't collided with each other, I thought to myself as I continued on with my round of golf. Looking back, I noticed a second bird landing next to the injured one, nudging its body with its beak as though to say, come on, you can do it, you can get up.

I began praying to God and to St Francis, the patron saint of animals, "please care for this bird, Your bird, this beautiful creature, that's lying on the ground, helpless and vulnerable to predators. Please let it heal and let it live the life it had." Looking up, it hit me that just moments before, this bird had been flying around with the others but now it has an injured wing such that, it may actually die. No, it won't die. It'll be fine just like I said it would, it will be ok. It also occurred to me that something quick and traumatic could happen to me or to anyone I love at any moment. One minute, everything is fine, and the next, it's not.

But just how does my being rich help the bird? It doesn't. It's God's help and St Francis' help that is needed. I prayed hard for this robin.

So why do I want to be rich? Well, unlike this bird, some people can actually be helped with money, giving them new leases on life and I would like to share that with them.

"Money is not the root of all evil, Dear," Grandma told me repeatedly, "greed is."

Grandma was very clear that having money was not an evil thing at all. But what did Grandma know about that, I wondered? After all, she never had much of it.

"It's much harder to share what you have when you don't have much than it is when you have lots," she advised. "When you only have a little bit for yourself, you are tempted to keep it, but that is the wrong thing to do.

You must share it with those who are in need and then it will come back to you. Maybe the money itself won't come back to you, but the benefit of the good deed will because you will be doing God's work when you help him to heal His people. The world has enough of everything in it for everyone when we share, but it does not have enough it in when greed is in control. Then there will be those who will go without while a few will have so much. These are the people who have to share their wealth so others may live. Start by sharing your wealth at home and then it will grow and prosper for the whole world to enjoy. If you want peace on earth, then start with peace at home. Do not be greedy with what you have, but rather, share it. Take that with you to your grave." And so Grandma did.

My grandmother tried to teach me about the power of prayer but it wasn't until I was much older that I actually experienced it in its entirety. Going to church with Grandma was sometimes tedious and hard to do and yet at other times, it was the easiest thing in the world. On good days, going to church gave me energy, lifted my spirits and gave me a deep feeling of being healed. But it was on those other days when I wasn't feeling quite so light hearted and didn't have an abundance of energy that were the hardest to make myself go to church. I learned later in life that those were the days I needed the most healing.

Grandma said that having a green thumb and a green lifestyle sometimes meant that she had to give her energy to the plants that were struggling and needed nurturing to live. She showed me the evergreen tree in her backyard that had been transplanted the month before and in the move, the root system had been damaged so the brilliant green branches had turned to a crisp dark brown leaving the untrained eye to believe the tree was dead. But deep within the branches and only after some water had been poured on it with the watering can, could the experienced believer see the tiny branches that were growing deep within the tree. This, my grandmother explained, was new life and new energy. It was the tree being healed and with care, it would come back to full life. Patience would be the virtue most required in this case; patience with loving tender care.

"Nothing will be impossible for you, my grandchild, if you learn to give loving tender care and then have the patience to watch it grow. You must plant the seeds of life, tend to it as God will have you do, helping it through it's difficult times of too little water, too much water, too much sun, not enough sun, bugs that eat the roots and leaves, and all the while praying to God for help, talking to your plant. Take this tree, for example. Evergreens like cooler temperatures and lots of moisture on the branches, so during a hot day, you can help it out by taking the watering can down to the cool stream below, filling it with fresh water and gently pouring the spring water over the tree. The tree will cool down and get a drink of water at the same time. It's like us humans; on a hot day, we need to drink lots of water and then our core temperature will decrease and we'll stay hydrated and healthy. This tree will like a drink too and over time, it will grow. The broken roots will heal and the tree will begin to grow from the inside out. Once the healing takes place on the inside, then healing will show on the outside where you will see it and eventually, the whole tree will become beautiful again. We'll help it out by cutting off the dried out branches but only once we know that those branches will never again produce life."

It was through these stories and analogies how I related church and God to healing. The older I got the more experienced I became in recognizing God's work in everything we do, say and live through. God spoke through Grandma in her words and in her actions with Grandma allowing this to be by always keeping her faith. In the bible under Romans, 1:16 &17 (ESV), Grandma read, 'For I am not ashamed of the gospel, for it is the power of God for salvation to everyone who believes….the righteous shall live by faith.' And it was this faith that my grandmother kept all her life and had it in all she did. She believed in God, she believed in people and she believed in her plants. She believed she was a vessel that God could use to do His work and that work showed through her gardens. All who needed food to eat were welcomed to come to Grandma's gardens to eat what they needed and she always had enough because the gardens continued to grow.

"That's what gardens do, Emma; they grow. A prolific garden is something that should be prayed for and then well tended to. If you fuss too much with it, then the plants will not grow because they may be over watered, or stepped on, or worse, you may pull them out thinking they're weeds when they're very young , but if you ignore the garden, then it will not grow either. The weeds will take over, the soil will become hard, dry and cracked and the new growth will shrivel up and fall to the ground. Either way, the garden will not feed you because you have not fed the garden," were lasting words I heard from my beautiful grandmother, the beautiful rose.

32

CONDEMNED

"Precious in the sight of the Lord, is the death of His saints."
-- Psalm 116:15

CONDEMNED! The word hit me like a ton of bricks and I felt like I had just been run over by a truck.

It was late fall and I had finished my shopping for the day. As I approached Grandma's house, I fondly thought back to all those times I spent with her growing up and visiting with her after school, where she lived so close to the schools I attended. On those days I went to Grandma's, she lifted my spirits by talking with me about my day, my friends and about the challenges that every teenager encounters at school along the way; things like smoking, drugs, sex, and skipping classes. But the things I liked talking about the most were around the subjects of getting onto sports teams, books I had to read for English class discussing the characters in them, hairstyles, makeup and fashion. I was naturally good in language and art classes but had to work at math and sciences, yet it was in the math and sciences, that I chose my career. Perhaps that was my first real mistake. My job at the bank had me crunching numbers and focusing on actuarial sciences predicting outcomes of financial gains and losses, mind boggling, and yet at the same time, boring stuff. My natural inclination was to mingle with the bankers, planning and strategizing for outcome and results. I preferred the people interaction part of banking and not so much the desk job sitting at the computer working on spreadsheets. But that was what I did and so when my job ended, I was not so sad as I might have been.

But the day I drove to her house and saw the sign on my grandmother's door, the sign with the word Condemned on it, I fell apart. At first, my vision blurred, and then I felt as though I were in a dream with everything swirling around me in slow motion and the surrounding sounds quieted down so I was oblivious to them. As I tried to step away from the door, I nearly lost my footing my legs were so weak. My breathing stopped and I saw silver flashes of stars within my eyes. So many, in fact, that to this day whenever I see Christmas ornaments that have silver stars or snowflake patterns on them, I feel faint. I remember this crisp late autumn day when the leaves were gone from their trees leaving their branches totally naked and exposed to the cold winter about to come, and I vividly remember wondering where my grandmother was. But I already knew. And with tears welling up in my eyes, I began to feel the warmth filling me even though now I was lying on the cold wooden floor of the porch hugging my coat close to my body, crying a hard painful cry. Choking up in my throat were tears of such pain and agony. I was both cold and warm at the same time. Never in my life had I prepared myself for this day and for it to happen so abruptly, and so without warning, was more harshness than I could bear.

Lying on this cold floor of the porch was where my future husband found me. Neither he nor I were to know of our fates together brought on that day by my precious grandmother's death, but the warmth I was feeling then from the touch of his hand on my shoulder felt heavenly to me.

Later that evening after I had rested, I watched the news not really wanting to hear it, but was more compelled by it than anything else. I wanted to know if the whole world was going to see what I already knew. I wanted to see for myself if her picture was the way I remembered her. And I wanted to hear how the newscaster portrayed the story and if they were empathetic or coldly distant. And yet, I couldn't quite tune into the TV because deep within my soul, I didn't care what the world saw. I only cared about what I knew to be true and I cared about preserving all my memories just the way I had them stored in my mind. And so, instead, I went to bed and slept in a deep slumber until the birds of the dawn chirped me awake into the sunlight of the next day and into the rest of my life.

And now, Christmas music with strings and pianos, reminds me of the funeral music that was played at my grandmother's eulogy. Very beautiful, calming and serene with tranquility built in to comfort the soul.

So it is with love, comfort and peace that at this time of year, Christmas, I think about the giving Grandma gave, both to people and animals, reminding me to always give of myself even when I have very little.

"This is when it will be the hardest to give because you will want to keep it for yourself, but when you share it, it will come back to you in dividends," Grandma whispered to me while wrapping her arms around my body in spirit. And dividends was I word I could understand.

"Now let's go bake some Christmas cookies,' I said to my own two children.

The End

EPILOGUE

"Let food be thy medicine and medicine be thy food."
-- Hippocrates

No matter what anyone said or believed, I knew my grandmother had been taken care of for her entire life. I knew she had been rewarded for her kindness and had always been protected here on earth. My only hope was that I would be able to emulate my grandmother's life with my own acts of kindness and consideration for others.

I imagined my grandmother with me every day throughout my adult life often thinking about what she would have said had she been alive to talk and grow older with me. With introspection, I could reach her teachings and use them every day, so much so, I was never alone. Grandma didn't leave me; she left me with her legacy of growing healthy gardens and of appreciating good quality food for life, which is my inheritance. An inheritance I felt compelled to share.

INDEX OF RECIPES

R
Roast Beef Dinner, 176
Roasted Red Pepper Dip, 8

S
Spice Jar, 152
Stains on Clothes, 128
Sesame Oil Skin Wash, 198

T
Tomato Chips, 98

V
Vanilla Pudding, 64

W
Whipped Butter, 57

ABOUT THE AUTHOR

Rhonda and her husband live in Ontario in the Durham Region where she works and plays. She is active in the community and enjoys golf, mountain biking, skiing, hiking and kayaking.

Rhonda's artistic flair is evidenced by the details she applies to the things she does including building her gardens and growing her vegetable plants. Cooking from whole ingredients is a life choice Rhonda made early in her adult years during a time of working shifts that required her to maximize her nutrition intake. Physical exercise has been a constant in Rhonda's life for quite some time and helps to keep her fit.

She does speaking engagements and enjoys entertaining audiences with her stories.

Connect with Rhonda
Blog: http://www.invitalityliving.com

Thank you for reading my book. If you enjoyed it, please take a moment to leave me a review at your favorite retailer.

Thanks!

Rhonda Rose

www.ingramcontent.com/pod-product-compliance
Lightning Source LLC
Chambersburg PA
CBHW060054150626
46556CB00017BA/415